SILVERMANE

OTHER FIVE STAR WESTERNS BY ZANE GREY:

SILVERMANE

A WESTERN QUARTET

ZANE GREY®

FIVE STAR

A part of Gale, Cengage Learning

GALE
CENGAGE Learning·

Detroit • New York • San Francisco • New Haven, Conn • Waterville, Maine • London

GALE
CENGAGE Learning

LIBRARY OF CONGRESS CATALOGING-IN-PUBLICATION DATA

Grey, Zane, 1872–1939.
  Silvermane : a western quartet / by Zane Grey. — 1st ed.
    p. cm.
  ISBN 978-1-4328-2624-6 (hardcover) — ISBN 1-4328-2624-7
(hardcover)
    1. Western stories. I. Title.
PS3513.R6545S55 2013
813'.52—dc23   2012032737

First Edition. First Printing: January 2013.
Published in conjunction with Golden West Literary Agency.
Published by Five Star™ Publishing, a part of Gale, Cengage Learning
Find us on Facebook– https://www.facebook.com/FiveStarCengage
Visit our website– http://www.gale.cengage.com/fivestar/
Contact Five Star™ Publishing at FiveStar@cengage.com

Printed in Mexico
1 2 3 4 5 6 7 17 16 15 14 13

ADDITIONAL COPYRIGHT INFORMATION

CONTENTS

FOREWORD
BY JON TUSKA

Zane Grey was born Pearl Zane Gray in Zanesville, Ohio on January 31, 1872. He was graduated from the University of Pennsylvania in 1896 with a degree in dentistry. He conducted a practice in New York City from 1898 to 1904, meanwhile striving to make a living by writing. He met Lina Elise Roth in 1900 and always called her Dolly. In 1905 they were married. With Dolly's help, Grey published his first novel himself, *Betty Zane* (Charles Francis Press, 1903), a story based on certain of his frontier ancestors. Eventually closing his dental office, Grey moved with Dolly into a cottage on the Delaware River, near Lackawaxen, Pennsylvania. It is now a national landmark.

Although it took most of her savings, it was Dolly Grey who insisted that her husband take his first trip to Arizona in 1907 with C.J. "Buffalo" Jones, a retired buffalo hunter who had come up with a scheme for crossing the remaining bison population with cattle. Actually Grey could not have been more fortunate in his choice of a mate. Dolly Grey assisted him in every way he desired and yet left him alone when he demanded solitude; trained in English at Hunter College, she proof-read every manuscript he wrote and polished his prose; she managed all financial affairs and permitted Grey, once he began earning a good income, to indulge himself at will in his favorite occupations: hunting, fishing, sailing, and exploring the Western regions.

After his return from that first trip to the West, Grey wrote a memoir of his experiences titled *The Last of the Plainsmen* (Outing, 1908) and followed it with his first Western romance, *The Heritage of the Desert* (Harper, 1910). Due to editorial changes and omissions made by Ripley Hitchcock, Grey's editor at Harper & Bros., that novel has now been restored as *Desert Heritage* (Five Star, 2010), the text taken from Zane Grey's holographic manuscript. The profound effect that the desert had had on him was vibrantly captured in this story, so much so that, after all of these years, it still comes alive for a reader. In a way, too, it established the basic pattern Grey would use in much of his subsequent Western fiction. The hero, Jack Hare, is an Easterner who comes West because he is suffering from tuberculosis. He is rejuvenated by the arid land. The heroine is Mescal, desired by all men but pledged by the Mormon Church to a man unworthy of her. Mescal and Jack fall in love, and this causes her to flee from Snap Naab, for whom she will be a second wife. Snap turns to drink, as will many another man rejected by heroines in other Grey Western romances, and finally kidnaps Mescal. The most memorable characters in this novel, however, are August Naab, the Mormon patriarch who takes Hare in at his ranch, and Eschtah, Mescal's grandfather, a Navajo chieftain of great dignity and no less admirable than Naab, and the equines, Black Bolly and Silvermane. The principal villain—a type not too frequently encountered in Grey's Western stories with notable exceptions such as *Desert Gold* (Harper, 1913), now restored as *Shower of Gold* (Five Star, 2007)—is Holderness, a Gentile and the embodiment of the Yankee business spirit that will stop at nothing to exploit the land and its inhabitants for his own profit. Almost a century later, he is still a familiar figure in the American West, with numerous bureaucratic counterparts in various federal agencies. In the end Holderness is killed by Hare, but then Hare is also capable of pardoning a man who has done wrong if there is a chance for his reclamation, a theme Grey shared with Max Brand.

The first story is this collection is "Silvermane." It is concerned with the efforts of two seasoned mustangers, Lee and Cuth Stewart, brothers, to capture the wild stallion Silvermane in the Sevier range country. A bounty of $500 has been placed on the stallion. Although it can stand alone as a story, it was actually a fragment from what was to be a novel about mustangers, a false start, if you will. The fragment is not dated, but it was probably written a year or two after *Desert Heritage*, since Silvermane in it is quite definitely the same Silvermane present in the novel. Black Bolly, with her name changed to Black Bess, is also quite the same mare. In *Desert Heritage*, when Black Bolly whistles as the men are pursuing Silvermane, August Naab asks: " 'Now, boys, did she whistle for Silvermane, or to warn him . . . which?' " The Stewart brothers in "Silvermane" wonder the same thing about Black Bess—is her loyalty to them, or to the wild stallion?

Zane Grey eventually did write his story of mustangers in pursuit of a wild stallion, this time named Panguitch. His title for it was *Panguitch*, but this title was changed to "Wild Horse Mesa" when the story appeared as a twelve-part serial in *The Country Gentleman* (4/19/24–7/5/24). *Panguitch*, based on Zane Grey's holographic manuscript, will appear as he wrote it in a Five Star edition in January, 2015.

Grey had trouble finding a book publisher for his early work, and it came as a considerable shock to him when his next novel after *Desert Heritage*, *Riders of the Purple Sage*, arguably the finest Western story he ever wrote, was rejected by the same editor who had bought *The Heritage of the Desert*. In desperation Grey asked the vice president at Harper & Bros. to read the new novel. Once he did, and his wife also read it, the book was accepted for publication, but with the understanding that Ripley

Hitchcock, who had initially rejected it, would make all the changes in the text he felt necessary. Here, too, a restored version, based on Zane Grey's original text, has been published as *Riders of the Purple Sage: The Restored Edition* (Five Star, 2005).

Riders of the Purple Sage is dominated by dream imagery and nearly all of the characters, at one time or another, are preoccupied with their dreams. For its hero Grey created the gunfighter, Lassiter, another enduring prototype, the experienced Westerner in contrast with the Eastern neophyte in *Desert Heritage*, Lassiter with his "leanness, the red burn of the sun, and the set changelessness that came from years of silence and solitude . . . the intensity of his gaze, a strained weariness, a piercing wistfulness of keen, gray sight, as if the man was forever looking for that which he never found." In this, as well, Lassiter is the prototype for all those searchers and wanderers found in Grey's later stories, above all John Shefford in *The Rainbow Trail* (Harper, 1915), restored as *The Desert Crucible* (Five Star, 2003), and Adam Larey in *Wanderer of the Wasteland* (Harper, 1923).

Hermann Hesse went East for inspiration in his dreaming; Zane Grey went West. "Yes," Hesse wrote in *Demian* (S. Fischer Verlag, 1919), "one must find his dream, for then the way is easy. However, there is no forever-enduring dream. Each dream surrenders to a new one, and one is able to hold fast to none of them." In *Riders of the Purple Sage*, life itself, the outer world, and human evil do not permit dreams to last indefinitely. Bishop Dyer dreams. Jane Withersteen dreams. Venters and Bess dream. Lassiter lives in a dream of vengeance. Lassiter in his relationship with Jane and her ward, Fay Larkin, fulfills an ancient dream of a family and, through his actions, fulfills his own dream by destroying Bishop Dyer. At the close, Lassiter, Jane, and Fay are alone, sealed in Surprise Valley. Hermann Hesse and Frederick Faust who wrote as Max Brand became familiar with Jungian ideas, and each for a time consulted with Jung. Grey could know nothing of the process of individuation in 1912 but what he grasped intuitively. For him, personal rebirth into a state of wholeness, the restoration of the Garden of Eden and a state of innocence, came only after the expenditure of passion and the vanquishing of evil. This would remain the psycho-drama underlying many of Zane Grey's finest Western stories.

In *Wanderer of the Wasteland*, Grey made Death Valley come alive in a way that is imperishable and provided this story with a character such as Dismukes, the old wise man, a prospector who, when young, was rejected by the woman he loved and so he came to wander in the desert. With each cache of gold he finds, Dismukes adds to his savings until, someday, he shall have a half million and will travel around the world before settling on a farm in the East. It is Dismukes who instructs Adam Larey in the ways in which a man can survive in the desert and how to reach a tribe of Indians who will teach Adam what more he needs to know. When Dismukes finds his fortune and does take his trip around the world, the money is only wasted. He learns that he must come back to the desert, to the only land he knows and loves, the only way of life he wants. His has been a spiritual odyssey, as is the case for so many of Grey's characters, and one where the final resolution is not accomplished through violence but through the achievement of wholeness within his own personality, or alternatively through a spiritual fragmentation that can be endured only with resignation. Such a character certainly fascinated Grey, and it is not surprising that he created another prospector very like him in Tappan in "Tappan's Burro." Tappan dreams, but he also sees the birth of Jenet, the sturdy burro who ventures with Tappan into the inferno of Death Valley and is able to lead Tappan through the midnight gale with its suffocating heat. The short novel was originally published in *Ladies Home Journal* (6/23), but for its appearance here, the text had been restored according to Zane Grey's holographic manuscript. The word "amaze" appears in it—"... he passed to amaze, and then to strident anger."—and I recall talking about that usage with Loren Grey, Zane Grey's younger son who had no idea why his father preferred "amaze" to the more proper "amazement," but Loren didn't like it. My only defense for his father's usage was that there was a definite precedent in English literature. Charlotte Brontë used "amaze" repeatedly in *Shirley* (1849), rather than "amazement," and perhaps that is where Zane Grey first encountered the usage.

Despite the problems he had with editors about his Mormon characters and their behavior, Grey persisted in featuring them. That is certainly true of "Cañon Walls," which is set in a Mormon community in the wilds of Utah Territory, a story first published as a three-part serial in *Ladies' Home Journal* (10/30–12/30). Smoke Bellew is on the dodge and finds safety, working at the Keitch farm in Cañon Walls Valley. The reader is told about Bellew: "It had been a shock, however, to find that two of Mrs. Keitch's Sunday callers, openly courting Rebecca's hand, already had wives. *By golly, I ought to marry her myself,* declared Monty with heat, as he soliloquized to himself beside his fire, and then he laughed at his dreaming conceit. He was only the hired help to Rebecca."

"Silvermane" was obviously not intended by Zane Grey for publication, and it wouldn't have appeared at all in any form had Loren Grey not been able to find only two installments of the magazine serial, "The Lone Star Rangers," which had first appeared in *All-Story Cavalier Weekly* (5/9/14–5/23/14). It was this first-person narrative that had been rewritten by Ripley Hitchcock and added to the first half of Zane Grey's rejected *The Last of the Duanes* to form the bowdlerized *The Lone Star Ranger* (Harper, 1915), more Hitchcock's book than Zane

Grey's. It was Loren Grey's idea to put the two serial install-ments, retitled "The Rustlers of Pecos County," together with the "Silvermane" fragment to form a Zane Grey original paperback duo, *The Rustlers of Pecos County and Silvermane* (Belmont Tower, 1979) edited by Loren Grey. Fortunately the authentic texts of *Last of the Duanes* (Five Star. 1996) and *Rangers of the Lone Star* (Five Star, 1997) have now been published as the author wrote them.

Neither "Silvermane" nor "Tappan's Burro" were ever filmed, but "Cañon Walls" served as the basis for the screenplay by Gordon Rigby and Sidney Mitchell for *Smoke Lightning* (Fox, 1933) directed by David Howard and starring George O'Brien and Nell O'Day. If you should happen to see the film, you will realize that in reality the only thing retained from the source was that O'Brien's first name is Smoke. Much screen time is spent on developing the relationship between Smoke and Betsy King Ross, a nine-year-old rodeo star who was beginning her short-lived film career. The Mormon background is no more present in this film than it has been in any of the five filmed versions of *Riders of the Purple Sage*.

Despite the difficulties Zane Grey encountered from the beginning in getting his Western stories published as he wrote them, what was published led to a degree of success that exceeded even Grey's wildest dreams. The magazine serials, the books, the motion picture versions—and Grey at one hundred and nine films still holds the world's record for cinematic deriva-tions based on the works of a single author—brought in a fortune. He had homes on Catalina Island, in Altadena, California, a hunting lodge in Arizona, and a fishing lodge on the Rogue River in Oregon.

Whatever his material prosperity, Grey continued to believe in the strenuous life. His greatest personal fear was that of growing old and dying. It was while fishing the North Umpqua

River in Oregon in the summer of 1937 that Grey collapsed from an apparent stroke. It took him a long time to recover use of his faculties and his speech. Cardiovascular disease was congenital on Grey's side of the family. Despite medical advice to the contrary, Grey refused to live a sedentary life. He was convinced that the heart was a muscle and the only way to keep it strong was to exercise it vigorously. Early in the morning on October 23, 1939, Dolly was awakened by a call from her husband. Rushing to his room, she found Grey clutching his chest. "Don't ever leave me, Dolly!" he pleaded. He lived until the next morning when, after rising and dressing, he sat down on his bed, cried out suddenly, and fell over dead.

It was Dolly Grey who had set up Zane Grey, Inc., while Zane Grey was alive, as a way of protecting Zane Grey's works and a portion of the income earned by those works. For much of the 1930s Dolly kept her husband on a budget where she controlled half the income of his works and their derivations. After Zane Grey died, she managed Zane Grey, Inc., but their elder son, Romer Grey, did most of the business negotiations and oversaw the continuing posthumous book publication of Zane Grey's fiction, of which there was a considerable amount that had not appeared in book form during Grey's lifetime. When Dolly Grey died, Romer Grey assumed the presidency of Zane Grey, Inc., a position he retained until his own death, when he was succeeded by Loren Grey. I had occasion in 1973 to have extensive conversations with Romer Grey about his father's works as well as the films based on them. Even then, not having access to Zane Grey's holographic manuscripts, it was obvious to me that other hands had been at work on these posthumous book versions than Zane Grey. An obvious example was "Open Range," a five-part serial that had appeared in *The Country Gentleman* (3/27–7/27) that had been substantially expanded when it appeared as *Valley of Wild Horses* (Harper,

1947). Romer Grey admitted to me that most of these manuscripts had been rewritten to make them more appealing to modern readers. This work was done primarily by Tom Curry who also was the ghost writer of numerous novels featuring Zane Grey characters published under the name Romer Zane Grey. Many years later, when Loren Grey and Zane Grey, Inc., became a client of Golden West Literary Agency, I went through each of these posthumous publications with him in order to determine who had anonymously rewritten them. "From Missouri," that had originally appeared in *McCall's Magazine* (7/26), had been rewritten by Tom Curry for its appearance in *The Ranger and Other Stories* (Harper, 1960) by Zane Grey. In a case like this, therefore, Zane Grey's holographic manuscript text not only differed from what *McCall's Magazine* had published originally but differed even more significantly from the version in the 1960 story collection. "From Missouri" was also filmed under the title *Life in the Raw* (Fox, 1933) directed by Louis King with a screenplay credited to Stuart Anthony but actually the work of Fox contract writers Gordon Rigby and Sidney D. Mitchell. The story was updated to 1933 and had automobiles. There was no schoolteacher. Claire Trevor played Judy Holloway who arrives in Arizona and does not realize that her brother, who she has come to visit, has lost his ranch. Her brother is involved in an express office robbery and Judy falls in love with George O'Brien, playing Jim Barry, who is arrested and falsely charged, escapes jail, meets up with Judy's outlaw brother, only for both to learn that Judy in the meantime has been kidnapped and must be rescued. Other than the incident of a young unmarried woman arriving in Arizona nothing from Grey's story made it to the screen.

A Zane Grey serial like "Open Range" has now been restored to what he wrote in *Open Range* (Five Star, 2002). The short stories collected in *Silvermane: A Western Quartet* have also been restored and appear now as the author wrote them. Even more than with Bret Harte, there has always been a tendency among literary critics to dismiss Zane Grey, although, unlike Harte, Grey at no point enjoyed any great favor with them while he was alive. But at least now, contemporary critics are able to evaluate Zane Grey's work as he wrote it. Very often in reviews these days Zane Grey's restored books are being genuinely and sincerely praised. It may have been a long time in coming, but at least what is being praised, and in a few cases blamed, is completely the author's own work untouched by the hands of others.

* * * * *

SILVERMANE

* * * * *

REWARD

*$500 will be paid for the death of Silvermane, leader of the
Sevier Range band of wild horses.*

Utah Cattle Company

This notice, with a letter, coming by stage and messenger to the
Stewarts, brightened what had been a dull prospect. Seldom
did a whole year's work capturing and corralling mustangs in
the cañons and on the plateaus pay them half as much as the
reward offered for this one stallion. The last season had been a
failure altogether. A string of pintos and mustangs, representing
months of hazardous toil, had climbed out of a cañon corral
and escaped to their old haunts. So on the strength of this opportunity the brothers packed and rode out of Fredonia across
the Arizona line into Utah. Two days took them beyond and
above the Pink Cliffs to the White Sage plateau and there the
country became new to them. From time to time a solitary
sheepherder, encountered shepherding his flock on a sage slope,
set them in the right direction, and on the seventh day they
reached Bain, the most southerly of the outposts of the big
Utah ranches. It consisted of a water hole, a corral, a log cabin,
and some range riders.

Generally mustang wranglers, men who lived by catching
mustangs, were held in contempt by the rangers and cowboys of
that iron-bound desert country. For mustangs were harder to
capture than deer, and, when captured and broken, brought

only a few dollars per head. The Stewarts however, though they had never earned any money to speak of, were famous all over the States. Stories of their wonderful pursuits, of their fleet mustangs and trailing hounds, had become campfire gossip on the ranges. So their advent at Bain aroused interest.

Lee and Cuth Stewart were tall, lean Mormons, as bronzed as desert Navajos, cool, silent, gray-eyed, still-faced. Both wore crude homespun garments much the worse for wear; boots that long before had given the best in them; laced leather wristbands, thin and shiny from contact with lassoes, and old gray slouch hats that would have disgraced cowboys. But this threadbare effect did not apply to the rest of the outfit. It showed a care that must have been in proportion to its hard use. And the five, beautiful racy mustangs, Black Bess in particular, proved that the Stewarts were Indians at the end of every day, for they certainly had camped where there were grass and water. The pack of hounds shared interest with the mustangs, and the leader, a great yellow, somber-eyed hound, Dash, by name, could have made friends with everybody had he felt inclined.

"We calculated, boys," held forth the foreman, "thet if anybody could round up Silvermane an' his bunch, it'd be you. Every ranger between here and Marypoole has tried an' failed. Silvermane is a rare stallion. He has more than hoss sense. It's the opinion of a good many of us fellers thet he wasn't born wild, an' thet he came into this country somewhere from Nevada. Fer two years now no one has been in rifle shot of him, fer the word has long since gone out to kill him. It's funny now to think how many rangers tried to corral him, trap him, run him down. He's been a heap of trouble to all the ranchers. He goes right into a bunch of hosses, fights an' kills the stallions, an' leads off what he wants of the rest. His band is scattered all over, an' no man can count 'em, but he's got at least five hundred hosses off the ranges. An' he's got to be killed or there won't be a safe grazin' spot left in Sevier County."

"How're we to know this hoss' trail when we do hit it?" asked Lee Stewart.

"You can't miss it. His right fore track has a notch thet bites in clean every step he takes. One of my rangers came in yesterday an' reported fresh sign of Silvermane at Cedar Springs, sixteen miles north along the red ridge there. An' he's goin' straight fer his hidin' place. Whenever he's been hard chased, he hits it back up there an' lays low fer a while. It's rough country, though I reckon it won't be to you cañon fellers."

"How about water?"

"Good chances fer water beyond Cedar, I reckon, though I don't know any springs. It's rare an' seldom any of us work up as far as Cedar. A scaly country up thet way . . . black sage, an' thet's all."

The Stewarts reached Cedar Springs that afternoon. It was a hot place; a few cedars, struggling for existence, lifted dead, twisted branches to the sun; a scant growth of grass greened the few shady spots, and a thin stream of water ran between glistening borders of alkali. A drove of mustangs had visited the spring since dawn and had obliterated all tracks made before.

While Cuth made camp, Lee changed his saddle to another mustang and rode up the ridge. His idea was to get a look at the country. The climb was not particularly steep, but it was long and took time, as he had to pick his way and zigzag the bare stony slopes. At last he reached the top, and caught a breath of cool wind. From where he stood, the ridge wound northward, growing rougher and higher. Ridges rolled to meet it from the left, while to the right it shelved off into the desert. Far northward a long black plateau leveled the horizon, and at each end a snow-capped peak shone coldly in the sun. Lee regretted that this vantage point was not higher, but he fixed in his mind as best he could the lay of the land, and returned to camp.

"We're jest on the edge of wild hoss country," he announced to Cuth. "Thet stallion probably had a picked bunch an' was drivin' them higher up. It's gettin' hot these days an' the browse is witherin'. I seen old deer sign on the ridge, an' cougar an' coyote sign trailin' after. They're all makin' fer higher up. I reckon we'll find 'em all on the Sevier plateau."

"Did you see the plateau?" asked Cuth.

"Plain. Near a hundred miles away yet. Jest a long flat ridge black with timber. Then there's the two snow peaks, Terrill an' Hilgard, pokin' up their cold noses. I reckon the plateau rises off these ridges, an' the Sevier River an' the mountains are on the other side. So we'll push on fer the plateau. We might come up with Silvermane an' his bunch."

All the next day they rode up the hard-packed trail winding along the base of the ridge. It was a long, gradual ascent, with the ridge ever growing rockier and more rugged, and the desert slipping below. Cedar trees flourished toward the close of the day's march and then merged thin yellow-green with the fresh dark green of the piñons. Sunset found them halting at a little water hole among a patch of cedars and boulders. First Cuth slipped the packs and Lee measured out the oats. On a hard trail the brothers always packed grain for their mounts. The fact that the mustangs when eating grain were also eating the profits of a trip never entered into the Stewarts' calculations. The horses first, then the hounds, and then themselves—that was the way of the mustang wranglers. Having ministered to the wants of their dumb friends, Lee and Cuth set about getting supper for themselves. Cuth had the flour and water mixed to a nicety and Lee had the Dutch oven on some red-hot coals when, moved by a common instinct, they stopped work and looked up.

The five mustangs were not munching their oats; their heads

were up. Black Bess, the keenest of the quintet, moved rest-lessly, and then took a few steps toward the opening in the cedars.

"Bess!" called Lee sternly. The mare stopped.

"She's got a scent," whispered Cuth, reaching for his rifle. "Mebbe it's a cougar."

"Mebbe, but I never knowed Bess to go lookin' up one. . . . *Hist!* Look at Dash."

The yellow hound had risen from among his pack and stood warily shifting his nose. He sniffed the wind, turned around and around, and slowly stiffened with his head pointed up the ridge. The other hounds caught something, at least the manner of their leader, and became restless.

"Down, Dash, down," said Lee, and then with a smile to Cuth: "Did you hear it?"

"Hear what?"

"Listen."

The warm breeze came down in puffs from the ridge; it rustled the cedars and blew fragrant whiffs of smoke into the hunters' faces and presently it bore a whistle, a low prolonged whistle. Cuth rose noiselessly to his feet and stood still. So horses, hounds, and men waited, listening. The sound broke the silence again, much clearer, a keen, sharp whistle. And the third time it rang down from the summit of the ridge, splitting the air, strong, trenchant, the fiery shrill whistle of a challenging stallion. Black Bess reared an instant straight up, and came down quivering.

"Look," whispered Lee tensely.

On the very summit of the bare ridge stood a noble horse clearly silhouetted against the purple and gold of sunset sky. He was an iron-gray, and he stood wild and proud, his long silver-white mane waving in the wind.

"Silvermane!" exclaimed Cuth.

He stood there one moment, long enough to make a picture that would never be forgotten by the wild-horse hunters, then moved back along the ridge and disappeared. Other horses, blacks and bays, showed above the sage for a moment, and they, too, passed out of sight.

"I couldn't never shoot that stallion," whispered Lee.

"No more could I," replied Cuth. "Now, what do you make of thet whistlin'?"

"Jest grazin' along easy-like. The wind sure favors us. He came to the hilltop an' jest snorted down, like a stallion will, to let anything as might be there know he could lick it. Thet whistle of his was jest plain fight. But Lord! Wasn't he a beauty? I never seen such a hoss, never, an' never any as could come near him."

"He sure was pretty. An', Lee, to my way of thinkin' he jest might hev winded our mustangs, Bess, anyhow. You know how we've had proof of scents between hosses as passed all our understandin'. Bess might need watchin'."

Lee shook his head gravely. "Mebbe. It was kinder strange. But you know, if we can't trust Bess, we can't never trust a hoss again. I reckon we'd better lay low tonight, keep the hounds an' hosses in, an' get an early start fer the next water hole. Thet bunch'll drink tomorrow or next day if they ain't scared."

Before daylight the brothers were up and at dawn filed out of the cedar grove. A band of coyotes caused some apprehension, as they followed yelping and barking, and might have alarmed the wild mustangs. The rising sun, however, soon sent the coyotes back to their lairs, allowing the hunters to proceed in a silence that satisfied them. The trained horses scarcely rattled a stone, and the hounds trotted ahead, unmindful of foxes and rabbits brushed out of the sage.

The morning passed and the afternoon waned. Green willows began to skirt the banks of a sandy wash and the mustangs sniffed as they smelled water. Presently the Stewarts entered a rocky corner refreshingly bright and green with grass, trees, and flowers, and pleasant with the murmur of bees and fall of water. A heavily flowing spring gushed from under a cliff and dashed down over stones to form a pool, then ran out to seep away and lose itself in the sandy wash. Flocks of blackbirds chattered around the pool and rabbits darted everywhere.

"It'd take a hull lot of chasin' to drive a mustang from comin' regular to that spring," commented Cuth.

"Sure, it's a likely place, an' we can throw up a corral here in short order."

They hobbled the mustangs, got supper, and then set to work on the corral. The plan was to build a circular fence around the pool and to leave an opening at the most favorable point, which was a wide beaten trail. By nightfall they had the pool enclosed except on the upper side where the water tumbled over a jumble of rocks, a place no horse could climb out, and on the lower side, where they left the opening for the gate. The gate was the important part and now presented a problem.

"We can't do no more tonight," said Lee, "an' we'll hev to take chances on Silvermane comin' down to drink tonight. Mebbe it'll be a couple of days before he comes, an' thet'll give us time to fix up a gate an' weak places in the fence."

All that night Lee and Cuth lay under the shadow of the corral, waiting and watching. The next morning they climbed the ridge and brought down three long pine poles. These they fashioned into a gate, and as it was found impossible to swing such a ponderous affair they concluded to let it lie flat before the opening, to be raised quickly after the wild mustangs had gone in to drink. In the afternoon the hunters slept with only Dash on guard; at nightfall they were ready and waiting for their quarry. What little breeze there was favored their position, and the night promised to be clear and starlit. In the early hours a prowling coyote bawled lonesomely, and deer came down to drink. Later soft-footed animals slipped with pad-like tread over the spring. At midnight the breeze failed and a dead stillness set in. It was not broken until the after part of the night, and then suddenly by the shrill piercing neigh of a mustang. The Stewarts raised themselves sharply and looked at each other in the starlight.

"Did you hear thet?" asked Lee.

"I jest did. Sounded like Bess."

"It was Bess, darn her black hide. She never did thet before."

"Mebbe she's winded Silvermane."

"Mebbe. But she ain't hobbled, an', if she'd whistle like thet fer him, she's liable to make off after him. Now what to do?"

"It's too late. I warned you before. We can't spoil what may be a chance to get the stallion. Let Bess alone. Many's the time she's had a chance to make off, an' didn't do it. Let's wait."

"Reckon it's all we can do now. If she called thet stallion it proves one thing . . . we can't never break a wild mare perfectly. The wild spirit may sleep in her blood, mebbe fer years, but some time it'll answer to. . . ."

"Shut up . . . listen," interrupted Cuth.

In the strained moments following, there was no sound, and no movement till Dash put his nose high, and turned slowly in a circle. His significant action meant to the hunters that he had passed the uneasy stage prior to the certainty of a scent, and was now baffled only by the direction.

"There," whispered Lee.

From far up on the ridge came down the faint rattling of stones.

"Mustangs . . . an' they're comin' down," replied Cuth.

Long experience had brought the brothers patience, but moments such as these, waiting in the shadow, had never come to be tranquil. Presently sharp clicks preceded the rattles, and, when these sounds grew together and became louder, the hearts of the hunters began to quicken. The sounds merged into a regular rhythmic tramp. It came down the ridge softened in the sandy wash below the spring, opened up again with a steady click and thump, and came straight for the corral.

"I see 'em," whispered Cuth. Lee answered by a pressure of his hand. It was an anxious moment, for the mustangs had to pass hunters and hounds before entering the gate. A black bobbing line wound out of the cedars. Then the starlight showed the line to be the mustangs marching in single file. They passed with drooping heads, hurrying a little toward the last, and unsuspiciously entered the corral gate.

"Twenty odd," whispered Lee, "but all blacks an' bays. Silvermane wasn't in thet bunch. Mebbe it wasn't his. . . ."

Among the cedars rose the peculiar halting thump of hobbled horses trying to cover ground, and following that snorts and crashings of brush and the pound of plunging hoofs. Then out of the cedars moved two shadows, the first a great gray horse with snowy mane, the second a small, graceful, shiny black mustang. Silvermane and Black Bess. The stallion, in the fulfillment of a conquest such as had made him famous on the wild ranges, was magnificent in action and wheeling about her. Whinnying, cavorting, he arched his splendid neck and pushed his head against her. His importunity was that of a master. Suddenly Bess snorted and whirled down the trail. Silvermane whistled one short blast of anger or terror, and thundered after. Black Bess was at last true to her desert blood. They vanished in the gray shadow of the cedars, as a stream of frightened mustangs poured out of the corral in a clattering roar.

Gradually the dust settled. Cuth looked at Lee and Lee looked at Cuth. For a while neither spoke. Cuth generously forbade saying to his brother: "I told you so." The failure of their plan was only an incident of horse wrangling and in no way discomfited them. But Lee was angry at his favorite.

"You was right, Cuth," he said. "Thet mare placed us at the finish. Ketched when she was a yearling, broke the best of any mustang we ever had, trained with us fer five years, an' helped down many a stallion . . . an' she runs off wild with thet big white-maned brute."

"Wal, they make a team, an' they'll stick," replied Cuth. "An' so'll we stick, if we have to chase them to the Great Salt Basin."

Next morning when the sun tipped the ridge rosy red, Lee put the big yellow hound on the notched track of Silvermane, and the long trail began. At noon the hunters saw the white-maned stallion heading his black across a rising plain, the first step of the mighty plateau stretching to the northward. As they climbed, grass and water became more frequently met with along the trail. For the most part Lee kept on the tracks of the mustang leader without the aid of the hound; Dash was used in the grass and on the scaly ridges where the trail was hard to find.

The succeeding morning Cuth spied Silvermane watching them from a high point. Another day found them on top of the plateau, among the huge brown pine trees and patches of snow and clumps of aspen. It took two days to cross the plateau— sixty miles. Silvermane did not go down but doubled on his trail. Rimming a plateau was familiar work for the hunters, and twice they came within sight of the leader and his band. Once a bunch of mustangs trooped out of a hollow and went over the wall, down on the back trail. Silvermane was not among them, and Dash did not split but kept on into the timber.

"He's broke up his band, cut out some," commented Lee.

"Wal, wait till he takes to weathered stone, then we'll see," replied Cuth.

Silvermane crossed the plateau again and then struck down into the valley. The trail was a long steep slope of weathered stone, and the pursuers zigzagged it with the ease of long practice in the cañon country. Many times the great stallion could be seen looking back. Evidently this steady, persistent pursuit nonplussed him. After these surveys he always plunged away in a cloud of dust. He crossed the Sevier Valley to the river, and turned back. The river was raging from thaws in the mountains. Then he struck up the valley. Another day put his pursuers high up among the slides of snow and silver spruces, and another across a divide into a rugged country of badlands, where barrens begin to show, and high mesas lift flat heads covered with patches of sage and grey-green cedars. So it went on day by day, but Silvermane turned back no more. He had marked a straight course, though every mile of it grew wilder. Sometimes for hours the hunters had him in sight, and always beside him was the little black they knew to be Bess.

There came a day when Silvermane cut out all of his band except Bess, and they went on alone. They made a spurt and lost the trailers from sight for two days. Then Bess dropped a shoe, and the pursuers came up. As she grew lamer and lamer, the stallion showed his mettle. He did not quit her, but seemed to grow more cunning as pursuit closed in on them. He chose the open places where he could see far, and browsed along, covering rods where formerly he had covered miles.

One day the trail disappeared on stony ground. And there Dash came in for his share. Behind him the Stewarts climbed a very high round-topped mesa, buttressed and rimmed by cracked cliffs. It was almost insurmountable. They reached the summit by a narrow watercourse, to find a wild and lonesome level enclosed by crags and gray walls. There were cedars and fine thin grass.

"Corralled," said Lee laconically as his keen eye swept the surroundings. "He's never been here before, an' there's no way off this mesa except by the back trail, which we'll close."

After fencing the split in the wall, the brothers separated and rode around the rim of the mesa. Silvermane had reached the end of his trail; he was in a trap. Lee saw the stallion flying like a gleam through the cedars, and suddenly came upon Black Bess limping painfully along. Lee galloped up, roped her, and led her, a tired and crippled mustang, back to the place selected for camp.

"Played out, eh?" said Cuth as he smoothed her dusty neck. "Wal, Bess, you can rest up an' help us ketch the stallion. Lee, there's good grazin' here, an' we can go down for water."

For their operations the hunters chose the highest part of the mesa, a level cedar forest. Opposite a rampart of the cliff wall they cut a curved line of cedars, dropping them close together to form a dense, impassable fence. This enclosed a good space free from trees. From the narrowest point, some twenty yards wide, they cut another line of cedars running diagonally back a mile into the center of the mesa. What with this labor and going down every day to take the mustangs to water, nearly a week elapsed. But time was of no moment to the Stewarts. Then, every day Bess was getting better, and Silvermane more restive. They heard him crashing through the cedars, and saw him standing in open spots, with his silver mane flying and his head turned over his shoulder watching, always watching.

"It'd be somethin' to find out how long thet stallion could go without waterin'," commented Lee. "But we'll make his tongue hang out tomorrow. An' jest fer spite we'll break him with Black Bess."

Daylight came cool and misty; the veils unrolled in the valleys; the purple curtains of the mountains lifted to the snow peaks, and became clouds, and then the red sun burned out of the east.

"If he runs this way," said Lee as he mounted Black Bess,

"drive him back. Don't let him in the corral till he's tired."

The mesa sloped slightly eastward and the cedar forest soon gave place to sage and juniper. Upon the extreme eastern point of the mesa Lee jumped Silvermane out of a clump of bushes. A race ensued for half the length of the sage flat, then the stallion made into the cedars and disappeared. Lee slowed down, trotting up the easy slope, and cut across somewhat to the right. Not long after he heard Cuth yelling and saw Silvermane tearing through the scrub. Lee proceeded to the point where he had left Cuth and waited. Soon the pound of hoofs thudded through the forest, coming nearer and nearer. Silvermane appeared straight ahead, running easily. At sight of Lee and the black mare he snorted viciously and, veering to the left, took to the open. Lee watched him with sheer admiration. The stallion had a beautiful stride and ran seemingly without effort. Then Cuth galloped up and reined in a spent and foam-flecked mustang.

"Thet stallion can run some," was his tribute.

"He sure can. Change hosses now an' be ready to fall in line when I chase him back."

With that Lee coursed away and soon crossed the trail of Silvermane and followed it at a sharp trot, threading in and out of the aisles and glades of the forest. He passed through to the rim, and circled half the mesa before he saw the stallion again. Silvermane stood on a ridge, looking backward. When the hunter yelled, Silvermane leaped as if he had been shot and plunged down the ridge. Lee headed to cut him off from the cedars. But the stallion forged to the front, gained the cedar level, and twisted in and out of the clumps of trees. Again Lee slowed down to save his mustang. Bess was warming up, and Lee wanted to see what she could do at close range. Keeping within sight of Silvermane, the hunter leisurely chased him around and around the forest, up and down the sage slopes, along the walls, at last to get him headed for the only open stretch on the mesa. Lee rode across a hollow and came out on the level only a few rods behind Silvermane.

"*Hi! Hi! Hi!*" yelled the hunter, spurring Bess forward like a black streak. Uttering a piercing snort of terror, the gray stallion lunged out, for the first time panic-stricken, and he lengthened his stride in a way that was wonderful to see. Then at the right moment Cuth darted in from his hiding place, whooping at the top of his voice and whirling his lasso. Silvermane won that race down the open stretch, but it cost him his best. At the turn he showed his fear and plunged wildly first to the left, then to the right. Cuth pushed him relentlessly, while Lee went back, tied up Black Bess, and saddled Billy, a wiry mustang of great endurance. Then the two hunters remorselessly hemmed Silvermane between them, turned him where they wished, at last to run him around the corner of the fence of cut cedars down the line through the narrow gate into the corral prepared for him.

"Hold here!" Lee cried at the gate. "I'll go in an' drive him around an' around till he's done, then, when I yell, you stand aside an' rope him as he goes out."

Silvermane ran around the triangular space, plunged up the steep walls, and crashed over the dead cedars. Then as sense and courage gave way more and more to terror he broke into desperate headlong flight. He ran blindly, and every time he passed the guarded gateway, his eyes were wilder and his stride more labored.

"*Hi! Hi! Hi!*" yelled Lee.

Cuth pulled out of the opening and hid behind the line of cedars, his lasso swinging loosely. Silvermane saw the vacated opening and sprang forward with a hint of his old speed. As he passed through, a yellow loop flashed in the sun, circling, narrowing, and he seemed to run right into it. The loop whipped close around the glossy neck and the rope stretched taut. Cuth's mustang staggered under the violent shock, went to his knees, but struggled up and held firmly. Silvermane reared aloft. There Lee, darting up in a cloud of dust, slid his lasso. The noose nipped the right foreleg of the stallion. He plunged down and for an instant there was a wild straining struggle, then he fell heaving and groaning. In a twinkling Lee sprang off and, slipping the rope that threatened to strangle Silvermane, replaced it by a stout halter, and made this fast to a cedar.

Whereupon the Stewarts stood back and gazed at their prize. Silvermane was badly spent, but not to a dangerous point; he was wet with foam but no fleck of blood showed; his superb coat showed scratches, but none cut the flesh. He got up after a while, panting heavily, and trembling in all his muscles. He was a beaten horse, but he showed no viciousness, only the wild fear of a trapped animal. He eyed Black Bess, and then the hunters, and last the halter.

"Lee, will you look at him . . . will you jest look at thet mane!" ejaculated Cuth.

"Wal," replied Lee, "I reckon thet reward, an' then some, can't buy him."

★ ★ ★ ★ ★

Tappan's Burro

★ ★ ★ ★ ★

I

Tappan gazed down upon the newly born little burro with something of pity and consternation. It was not a vigorous offspring of the redoubtable Jennie, champion of all the numberless burros he had driven in his desert prospecting years. He could not leave it there to die. Surely it was not strong enough to follow its mother, and to kill it was beyond him.

"Poor little devil," soliloquized Tappan. "Reckon neither Jennie nor I wanted it to be born. . . . I'll have to hold up in this camp a few days. You can never tell what a burro will do. It might fool us an' grow strong all of a sudden."

Whereupon Tappan left Jennie and her tiny, gray, lop-eared baby to themselves and leisurely set about making permanent camp. The water at this oasis was not much to his liking, but it was drinkable, and he felt he must put up with it. For the rest the oasis was desirable enough as a camping site. Desert wanderers like Tappan favored the lonely water holes. This one was up inside the bold brow of the Chocolate Mountains where rocky wall met the desert sand, and a green patch of palo verdes and mesquites proved the presence of water. It had a magnificent view down a many-leagued slope of desert growths, across the dark belt of green and shining strip of red that marked the Río Colorado, and on to the upflung Arizona land, range lifting to range until the saw-toothed peaks notched the blue sky.

Locked in the iron fastnesses of these desert mountains was

gold. Tappan, if he had any calling, was a prospector. But the lure of gold did not bind him to this wandering life any more than the freedom of it. He had never made a rich strike. About the best he could ever do was to dig enough gold to grubstake himself for another prospecting trip into some remote corner of the American Desert. Tappan knew the arid Southwest from San Diego to the Pecos River and from Picacho on the Colorado to the Tonto Basin. Few prospectors had the strength and endurance of Tappan. He was a giant in build, and at thirty-five had never yet reached the limit of his physical force.

With hammer and pick and magnifying glass, Tappan scaled the bare ridges. He was not an expert in testing minerals. He knew he might easily pass by a rich vein of ore. But he did his best, sure at least that no prospector could get more than he out of the pursuit of gold. Tappan was more of a naturalist than a prospector, and more of a dreamer than either. Many were the idle moments that he sat staring down the vast reaches of the valleys, or watching some creature of the wasteland, or marveling at the vivid hues of desert flowers.

Tappan waited two weeks at this oasis for Jennie's baby burro to grow strong enough to walk. The very day that Tappan decided to break camp he found signs of gold at the head of a wash above the oasis. Quite by chance, as he was looking for his burro, he struck his pick into a place no different from a thousand others there and hit into a pocket of gold. He cleaned the pocket out before sunset, the richer for several thousand dollars.

"You brought me luck," said Tappan to the little gray burro, staggering around its mother. "Your name is Jenet. You're Tappan's burro, an' I reckon he'll stick to you."

Jenet belied the promise of her birth. Like a seed in fertile ground, she grew. Winter and summer Tappan journeyed from one trading post to another, and his burro traveled with him. Jenet had an especially good training. Her mother had happened to be a remarkably good burro before Tappan had bought her. Tappan had patience; he found leisure to do things, and he had something of pride in Jenet. Whenever he happened to drop into Ehrenberg or Yuma or any freighting station, some prospector always tried to buy Jenet. She grew as large as a medium-size mule, and a three hundred pound pack was no load to discommode her.

Tappan, in common with most lonely wanderers of the desert, talked to his burro. As the years passed, this habit grew until Tappan would talk to Jenet just to hear the sound of his voice. Perhaps that was all that kept him human.

"Jenet, you're worthy of a happier life," Tappan would say as he unpacked her after a long day's march over the barren land. "You're a ship of the desert. Here we are, with grub an' water, a hundred miles from any camp. An' what but you could have fetched me here? No horse, no mule, no man. Nothin' but a camel, an' so I call you ship of the desert. But for you an' your kind, Jenet, there'd be no prospectors, an' few gold mines. Reckon the desert would be still an unknown waste. You're a great beast of burden, Jenet, an' there's no one to sing your praise." And of a golden sunrise, when Jenet was packed and ready to face the cool, sweet fragrance of the desert, Tappan was wont to say: "Go along with you, Jenet. The mornin's fine. Look at the mountains yonder callin' us. It's only a step down there. All purple an' violet! It's the life for us, my burro, an' Tappan's as rich as if all these sands were pearls." But sometimes, at sunset, when the way had been long and hot and rough, Tappan would bend his shaggy head over Jenet, and talk in a different mood. "Another day gone, Jenet, another journey ended . . . an' Tappan is only older, wearier, sicker. There's no reward for your faithfulness. I'm only a desert rat, livin' from

41

hole to hole. No home! No face to see! Only the ghost of memories. Some sunset, Jenet, we'll reach the end of the trail. An' Tappan's bones will bleach in the sands. An' no one will know or care."

When Jenet was ten years old, she would have taken the blue ribbon in competition with all the burros of the Southwest. She was unusually large and strong, perfectly proportioned, sound in every particular, and practically tireless. But these were not the only characteristics that made prospectors envious of Tappan. Jenet had the common virtues of all good burros magnified to an unbelievable degree. Moreover, she had sense and instinct that to Tappan bordered on the supernatural.

During these years Tappan's trail criss-crossed the mineral region of the Southwest. But as always the rich strike held aloof. It was like the pot of gold buried at the foot of the rainbow. Jenet knew the trails and the water holes better than Tappan. She could follow a trail obliterated by drifting sand or cut out by running water. She could scent at long distance a new spring on the desert or a strange water hole. She never wandered far from camp so that Tappan would have to walk far in search of her. Wild burros, the bane of most prospectors, held no charm for Jenet, and she had never yet shown any especial liking for a tame burro. This was the strangest feature of Jenet's complex character. Burros were noted for their habit of pairing off, and forming friendships for one or more comrades. These relationships were permanent. But Jenet still remained fancyfree.

Tappan scarcely realized how he relied upon this big, gray, serene beast of burden. Of course, when chance threw him among men of his calling, he would brag about her, but he had never really appreciated Jenet. In his way Tappan was a brooding, plodding fellow, not conscious of sentiment. When he bragged about Jenet, it was her great qualities upon which he dilated. But what he really liked best about her were the little things of every day.

During the earlier years of her training, Jenet had been a thief. She would pretend to be asleep for hours just to get a chance to steal something out of camp. Tappan had broken this habit in its incipiency. But he never quite altogether trusted her. Jenet was a burro. Jenet ate anything offered her. She could fare for herself or go without. Whatever Tappan had left from his own meals was certain to be rich dessert for Jenet. Every mealtime she would stand near the campfire, with one great long ear drooping, and the other standing erect. Her expression was one of meekness, of unending patience. She would lick a tin can until it shone resplendently. On long, hard, barren trails Jenet's deportment did not vary from that where the water holes and grassy patches were many. She did not need to have grain or grass. Brittle-bush and sage were good fare for Jenet. She could eat greasewood, a desert plant that protected itself with a sap as sticky as varnish and far more dangerous to animals. She could eat cactus. Tappan had seen her break off leaves of the prickly pear cactus and stamp upon them with her fore hoofs, mashing off the thorns, so that she could eat the succulent pulp. She liked mesquite beans, leaves of willow, and all the trailing vines of the desert. She could subsist in an arid wasteland where a man would have died in short order.

No ascent or descent was too hard or dangerous for Jenet, provided it was possible of accomplishment. She would refuse a trail that was impossible. She seemed to have an uncanny instinct both for what she could do, and what was beyond a burro. Tappan had never known her to fail on something that she stuck to persistently. Swift streams of water, always bugbears to burros, did not stop Jenet. She hated quicksand, but could be trusted to navigate it, if that were possible. When she stepped gingerly, with little inch steps, out upon thin crust of ice or salty crust of desert sinkhole, Tappan would know that it was safe, or she would turn back. Thunder and lightning, intense heat or bitter cold, the sirocco sandstorm of the desert, the white dust of the alkali wastes, these were all the same to Jenet.

One August, the hottest and driest of his desert experience, Tappan found himself working a most promising claim in the lower reaches of the Panamint Mountains on the northern slope above Death Valley. It was a hard country at the most favorable season; in August it was terrible. The Panamints were infested by various small gangs of desperadoes—outlaw claim-jumpers where opportunity afforded and out-and-out robbers, even murderers, where they could not get the gold any other way. Tappan had been warned not to go into this region alone, but he never heeded any warnings. The idea that he would ever strike a gold claim big enough to make himself an attractive target for outlaws seemed preposterous and not worth considering. Tappan had become a wanderer from the unbreakable habit of it. Much to his amazement he struck a rich ledge of free gold in a cañon of the Panamints, and he worked from daylight until dark. He forgot about the claim-jumpers, until one day he saw Jenet's long ears go up in the manner habitual with her when she saw strange men. Tappan watched the rest of that day, but did not catch a glimpse of any living thing. It was a desolate place, shut-in, red-walled, hazy with heat, and brooding with an eternal silence.

Not long after that Tappan discovered boot tracks of several men adjacent to his camp, and in an out-of-the-way spot that persuaded him that he was being watched by claim-jumpers who were not going to jump his claim in this torrid heat, but meant to let him dig the gold and then kill him! Tappan was not the kind of man to be afraid. He grew wrathful and stubborn. He had six small canvas bags of gold and did not mean to lose them. Still he grew worried. *Now what's best to do,* he pondered. *I needn't give it away that I'm wise. Reckon I'd better act natural.*

But I can't stay here longer. My claim's about worked out. An' these jumpers are smart enough to know it. I've got to make a break at night. What to do?

Tappan did not want to cache the gold, for in that case, of course, he would have to return for it. Still he reluctantly admitted to himself that this was the best chance to save it. Probably these robbers were watching him day and night. It would be most unwise to attempt escaping by going up over the Panamints. "Reckon my only chance is goin' down into Death Valley," soliloquized Tappan grimly. This alternative was not to his liking. Crossing Death Valley at this season was always perilous and never attempted in the heat of day. At this particular time of intense torridity, when the day heat was unendurable and the midnight furnace gales were blowing, it was an enterprise from which even Tappan shrank. Added to this were the facts that he was too far west of the narrow part of the valley, and, even if he did get across, he would find himself in the most forbidding and desolate region of the Funeral Mountains.

Thus thinking and planning, Tappan went about his mining and camp tasks, trying his best to act natural. But he did not succeed. It was impossible while expecting a shot at any moment to act as if there was nothing on his mind. His camp lay at the bottom of a rocky slope. A tiny spring of water made verdure of grass and mesquite, welcome green in all that stark iron nakedness. His campsite was out in the open, on the bench near the spring. The gold claim that Tappan was working could not be seen from any vantage point, either below or above. It lay back at the head of a break in the rocky wall. It had two virtues—one that the sun never got to it, and the other that it was well hidden. Once there, Tappan knew he could not be seen. This, however, did not diminish his growing uneasiness. Something sinister hung over him. The solemn stillness was a menace. The heat of the day appeared to be increasing to a

degree beyond his experience. Every few moments Tappan
would slip back through a narrow defile in the rocks and peep
from this covert at the camp. On the last of these occasions, he
saw Jenet out in the open. She stood motionlessly. Her long
ears were erect. In an instant Tappan became strung with thrilling excitement. His keen eyes searched every approach to his
camp, and at last in the gully below to the right he saw two men
crawling along from rock to rock. Jenet had seen them enter
that gully and was now watching for them to appear.

Tappan's excitement succeeded to a grimmer emotion. These
stealthy visitors were going to hide in ambush, and kill him as
he returned to camp. *Jenet, reckon what I owe you is a whole lot,*
mused Tappan. *They'd have got me sure. But now....* Tappan left
his tools and crawled out of his covert into the jumble of huge
rocks toward the left of the slope. He had a six-shooter. His rifle
he had left in camp. Tappan had seen only two men, but he
knew there were more than that, if not actually near at the moment, then surely not far away. His only chance was to worm
his way like an Indian down to camp. With the rifle in his possession he would make short work of the present difficulty.

Lucky Jenet's right in camp, thought Tappan. *It beats hell how
she does things.*

Tappan was already deciding to pack and hurry away. At this
moment, Death Valley did not daunt him. Yet the matter of
crawling and gliding along was work unsuited to his great
stature. He was too big to hide behind a little shrub or a rock,
and he was not used to stepping lightly. His hobnailed boots
could not be placed noiselessly upon the stones. Moreover, he
could not step without displacing little bits of weathered rock.
He was sure that keen ears not too far distant might have heard
him, yet he kept on, making good progress around that slope to
the far side of the cañon. Fortunately he headed up the gully
where his ambushers were stealing forward. On the other hand

this far side of the cañon afforded but little cover. The sun had gone down behind a huge red mass of the mountain. It had left the rocks so hot Tappan could not touch them with his bare hands.

He was about to stride out from his last covert and make a run for it down the rest of the slope, when, surveying the whole amphitheater below him, he espied the two men coming up out of the gully, headed toward his camp. They looked in his direction. Surely they had heard or seen him. But Tappan saw at a glance that he was closer to the camp. Without another moment of hesitation he plunged from his hiding place, down the weathered slope. His giant strides set the loose rocks sliding and rattling. The robbers saw him. The foremost yelled to the one behind him. Then they both broke into a run. Tappan reached the level of the bench and saw he could beat either of the robbers into the camp. Unless he were disabled! He felt the wind of a heavy bullet before he heard it strike the rocks beyond. Then followed the boom of a Colt. One of his enemies had halted to shoot. This spurred Tappan to tremendous exertion. He flew over the rough ground, scarcely hearing the rapid shots. He could no longer see the man who was firing, but the first one was in plain sight, running hard, not yet seeing he was out of the race. When he became aware of that, he halted and, dropping on one knee, leveled his gun at the running Tappan. The distance was scarcely sixty yards. His first shot did not allow for Tappan's speed. His second kicked up gravel in Tappan's face. Then followed three more shots in rapid succession. The robber divined that Tappan had a rifle in camp. He steadied himself, waiting for the moment when Tappan had to slow down and halt. As Tappan reached his camp and dived for his rifle, the robber took time for his last aim, evidently hoping to get a stationary target. But Tappan did not get up from behind his camp duffel. It had been a habit of his to pile his boxes of supplies and roll of bedding together and cover them with a canvas. He poked his rifle over the top of this and shot the robber. Then, leaping up, he ran forward to get sight of the second one. This man began to run along the edge of the gully. Tappan fired rapidly at him. The third shot knocked the fellow down. But he got up, and, yelling as if for succor, he ran off. Tappan got another shot off before he disappeared.

"Ahuh," grunted Tappan grimly. His keen gaze came back to survey the fallen robber, and then went out over the bench, across the inside mouth of the cañon. Tappan thought he had better utilize time to pack instead of pursuing the second robber. Reloading the rifle, he hurried out to find Jenet. She was coming into camp.

"Shore you're a treasure, old girl!" ejaculated Tappan.

Never in his life had he packed Jenet, or any other burro, so quickly. His last act was to drink all he could hold, fill his tin canteens, and make Jenet drink. Then, rifle in hand, he drove the burro out of camp, around the corner of red wall, to the wide gateway that opened down into Death Valley.

Tappan looked back more than he looked ahead, and he had traveled down a mile or more before he began to breathe easier. He had escaped the claim-jumpers. Even if they did show up in pursuit now, they could never catch him. Tappan believed he could travel faster and farther than any man of that ilk. But they did not show up. Perhaps the crippled robber had not been able to reach his comrades in time. More likely, however, the gang had no taste for a chase in that torrid heat.

Tappan slowed his stride. He was almost as wet with sweat as if he had fallen into the spring. The great beads rolled down his face, and there seemed to be little streams of fire trickling down his breast. Despite this, and his labored panting for breath, not until he halted in the shade of a rocky wall did he realize the heat. It was terrific. Instantly, then, he knew he was safe from pursuit, but he knew also that he faced a greater peril than that of robbers. He could fight evil men, but he could not fight this heat.

So he rested there, regaining his breath. Already thirst was acute. Jenet stood nearby, watching him. Tappan imagined the burro looked serious. A moment's thought was enough for Tappan to appreciate the gravity of his situation. He was about to go down into the upper end of Death Valley—a part of that country unfamiliar to him. He must cross it, and also the Funeral Mountains, at a season when a prospector who knew the trails and water holes would have to be forced to undertake it, but Tappan had no choice. His rifle was too hot to hold, so he stuck it in Jenet's pack, and, burdened only by a canteen of water, he set out, driving the burro ahead. Once he looked back up the wide-mouthed cañon. It appeared to smoke with red heat veils. The silence was oppressive.

Presently he turned the last corner that obstructed sight of Death Valley. Tappan had never been appalled by any aspect of the desert, but here he halted. Back in his mountain-walled camp the sun had passed behind the high domes, but here it still held most of the valley in its blazing grip. Death Valley looked a ghastly glaring level of white over which a strange, dull, leaden haze dropped like a blanket. Ghosts of mountain peaks appeared dim and vague. There was no movement of anything. No wind! The valley was dead. Desolation reigned supreme. Tappan could not see far toward either end of the valley. A few miles of white glare merged at last into a leaden pall. A strong odor, not unlike sulphur, seemed to add weight to the air.

Tappan strode on, mindful that Jenet had decided opinions of her own. She did not want to go straight ahead or to right or left, but back. That was the one direction impossible for Tappan, and he had to resort to a rare measure—that of beating her—but at last Jenet accepted the inevitable and headed down into the stark and naked plain. Soon Tappan reached the margin of the zone of shade cast by a mountain and was not so exposed to the sun. The difference seemed tremendous. He had been hot, oppressed, weighted. It was now as if he was burned through his clothes and had walked on red-hot sands.

When Tappan ceased to sweat and his skin became dry, he drank half a canteen of water, and slowed his stride. Inured to the desert hardship as he was, he could not long stand this. Jenet did not show any lessening of vigor. In truth, what she showed now was an increasing nervousness. It was almost as if she scented an enemy. Tappan never before had such faith in her. Jenet was equal to this task.

With that blazing sun on his back, Tappan felt he was being pursued by a furnace. He was compelled to drink the remaining half of his first canteen of water. Sunset would save him. Two more hours of such insupportable heat would lay him prostrate.

The ghastly glare of the valley took on a reddish tinge. The heat was blinding Tappan. The time came when he walked beside Jenet with a hand on her pack, for he could no longer endure the furnace glare. Even with closed eyes he knew when the sun sank behind the Panamints. That fire no longer followed him. The red left his eyelids.

With the sinking of the sun the world of Death Valley changed. It smoked with heat veils, but the intolerable constant burn was gone. The change was so immense that it seemed to have brought coolness.

In the twilight—strange, ghostly, somber, silent as death—Tappan followed Jenet off the sand, down upon the silt and borax level, to the crusty salt. Before dark, Jenet halted at a sluggish belt of fluid—acid, it appeared to Tappan. It was not deep, and the bottom felt stable, but Jenet refused to cross. Tappan trusted her judgment more than his own. Jenet headed to the left and followed the course of the strange stream.

Night intervened—a night without stars or sky or sound, hot, breathless, charged with some intangible current. Tappan dreaded the midnight furnace winds of Death Valley. He had never encountered them. He had heard prospectors say that any man caught in Death Valley when these gales blew would never get out to tell the tale, and Jenet seemed to have something on her mind. She was no longer a leisurely complacent burro. Tappan imagined Jenet seemed stern. Most assuredly she knew now which way she wanted to travel. It was not easy for Tappan to keep up with her, and ten paces ahead of him she was out of sight.

At last Jenet headed the acid wash, and turned across the valley into a field of broken salt crust, like the roughened ice of a river that had broken and jammed, then froze again. Impossible it was to make even a reasonable headway. It was a zone, however, that eventually gave way to Jenet's instinct for direction. Tappan had long ceased to try to keep his bearings. North, south, east, and west were all the same to him. The night was a blank—the darkness a wall—the silence a terrible menace flung at any living creature. Death Valley had endured them millions of years before living creatures had existed. It was no place for a man.

Tappan was now three hundred and more feet below sea level, in the aftermath of a day that had registered one hundred and forty-five degrees of heat. He knew when he began to lose thought and balance—when also the primitive directed his bodily machine—and he struggled with all his willpower to keep hold of his sense of sight and feeling. He hoped to cross the lower level before the midnight gales began to blow.

Tappan's hope was vain. According to record, once in a long season of intense heat, there came a night when the furnace winds broke their schedule and began early. The misfortune of

Tappan was that he had struck this night.

Suddenly it seemed that the air, sodden with heat, began to move. It had weight. It moved soundlessly and ponderously, but it gathered momentum. Tappan realized what was happening. The blanket of heat generated by the day was yielding to outside pressure. Something had created a movement of the hotter air that must find its way upward to give place to the cooler air that must find its way down. Tappan heard the first low, distant moan of wind, and it struck terror in his heart. It did not have an earthly sound. Was that a knell for him? Nothing was surer than the fact that the desert must sooner or later claim him as a victim. Grim and strong, he rebelled against the conviction.

That moan was a forerunner of others, growing louder and longer until the weird sound became continuous. Then the movement of wind was accelerated and began to carry a fine dust. Dark as the night was, it did not hide the pale sheets of dust that moved along the level plain. Tappan's feet felt the slow rise in the floor of the valley. His nose recognized the zone of borax and alkali and niter and sulphur. He had gotten into the pit of the valley at the time of the furnace winds.

The moan augmented to a roar, coming like a nightly storm through a forest. It was hellish—like the woeful tide of Acheron. It enveloped Tappan, and the gale bore down in thunderous volume, like a furnace blast. Tappan seemed to feel his body penetrated by a million needles of fire. He seemed to dry up. The blackness of night had a spectral whitish cast; the gloom was a whirling medium; the valley floor was lost in a sheeted, fiercely seeping stream of silt. Deadly fumes swept by, not lingering long enough to suffocate Tappan. He would gasp and choke—then the poison gas was gone in the gale. But hardest to endure was the heavy body of moving heat. Tappan grew blind, so that he had to hold to Jenet and stumble along. Every gasping breath was a tortured effort. He could not bear a scarf over his face. His lungs heaved like great leather bellows. His heart pumped like an engine short of fuel. This was the supreme test for his never-proven endurance, and he was all but vanquished.

Tappan's senses of sight and smell and hearing failed him. There was left only the sense of touch—a feeling of rope and burro and ground—and an awful insulating pressure upon all his body. His feet marked a change from salty plain to sandy ascent and then to rocky slope. The pressure of wind gradually lessened; the difference in air made life possible; the feeling of being dragged endlessly by Jenet at last ceased. Tappan went his limit and fell into oblivion.

When he came to, he was suffering bodily tortures. Sight was dim. But he saw walls of rocks, green growths of mesquite, tamarack, and grass. Jenet was lying down, with her pack flopped to one side. Tappan's dead ears recovered to a strange murmuring, babbling sound. Then he realized his deliverance. Jenet had led him across Death Valley, up into the mountain ranges, straight to a spring of running water.

Tappan crawled to the edge of the water and drank guardedly, a little at a time. He had to quell the terrific craving to drink his fill. Then he crawled to Jenet and, loosening the ropes of her pack, freed her from its burden. Jenet got up, apparently none the worse for her ordeal. She gazed mildly at Tappan, as if to say: "Well, I got you out of that hole."

Tappan returned her gaze. Were they only man and beast, alone in the desert? She seemed magnified to Tappan, no longer a plodding, stupid burro.

"Jenet, you . . . saved my life," Tappan tried to enunciate. "I'll never . . . forget."

Tappan was struck then to a realization of Jenet's service. He was unutterably grateful. Yet, the time came when he did forget. . . .

II

Tappan had a weakness common to all prospectors, but intensified in him. Any tale of a lost gold mine would excite his interest, and well-known legends of lost miners always obsessed him. Peg-Leg Smith's lost gold mine had lured Tappan to no less than half a dozen trips into the terrible, shifting sand country of southern California. There was no water near the region said to hide this mine of fabulous wealth. Many prospectors had left their bones to bleach white in the sun and at last be buried by the ever-blowing sands. Upon the occasion of Tappan's last escape from this desolate and forbidding desert he had promised Jenet never to undertake it again. It seemed Tappan promised the faithful burro a good many things. It had become a habit.

When Tappan had a particularly hard time or perilous adventure, he always took a dislike to the immediate country where it had happened. Jenet had dragged him across Death Valley, through incredible heat and the midnight furnace winds of that strange place, and he had promised her he would never forget how she had saved his live, nor would he ever go back to Death Valley. He crossed the Funeral Mountains, worked down through Nevada, and crossed the Río Colorado above Needles, and entered Arizona. He traveled leisurely, but he kept going, and headed southeast toward Globe. There he cashed one of his six bags of gold and indulged in the luxury of a completely new outfit. Even Jenet appreciated this fact, for the old outfit could scarcely hold together.

Tappan had the other five bags of gold in his pack, and after hours of hesitation he decided he would not cash them and trust the money to a bank. He would take care of them. For him the value of this gold amounted to a small fortune. Many plans suggested themselves to Tappan, but in the end he grew weary of them. What did he want with a ranch, or cattle, or an outfitting store, or any of the businesses he now had the means to buy? Towns soon palled on Tappan. People did not long please him. Selfish interest and greed seemed paramount everywhere. Besides, if he acquired a place to take up his time, what would become of Jenet? That question decided him. He packed the burro and once more took to the trails.

A dimly purple, lofty range called alluringly to Tappan. The Superstition Mountains! Somewhere in that purple mass laid the famous treasure called the Lost Dutchman gold mine. Tappan had heard the story often. A Dutch prospector had struck gold in the Superstitions. He had kept the location secret. When he had run short of money, he would disappear for a few weeks, and then return with bags of gold. His strike assuredly had been a rich one. No one ever could trail him or get a word out of him. Time passed. A few years made him old. During this time he conceived a liking for a young man and eventually confided that someday he would tell him the secret of his gold mine. He had drawn a map of the landmarks adjacent to his mine, but he was careful not to put on paper directions how to get there. It chanced that he suddenly fell ill and saw his end was near. Then he summoned this young man who had been so fortunate as to win his regard. Now this individual was a ne'er-do-well, and upon this occasion of his being summoned he was half drunk. The dying Dutchman produced his map and gave it with verbal directions to the young man. Then he died. When the recipient of this fortune recovered from the effects of liquor, he could not remember all the Dutchman had told him. He tortured himself to recall names and places. The mine was up in the Superstition Mountains. He never remembered quite where. He never found the lost mine, although he spent his life at it and died trying. The story passed into legend as the Lost Dutchman Mine.

Tappan had his try at finding it. For him the shifting sands of the southern California desert or even the barren and desolate Death Valley were preferable to this Superstition Range. It was a harder country than the Pinacate of Sonora. Tappan hated cactus, and the Superstitions were full of it. The huge saguaro stood everywhere, the giant cacti of the Arizona plateaus, tall like branchless trees, fluted and columnar, beautiful and fascinating to gaze upon, but obnoxious to prospector and burro.

One day from a north slope, Tappan saw afar a wonderful country of black timber that zigzagged for many miles in yellow winding ramparts of rock. This he took to be the rim of the Mogollon Mesa, one of Arizona's freaks of Nature. Something called to Tappan. He was forever victim to yearnings for the unattainable. He was tired of heat, glare, dust, bare rock, and thorny cactus. The Lost Dutchman gold mine was a myth. Besides, he did not need any more gold.

Next morning Tappan packed Jenet and worked down off the north slope of the Superstition range. That night about sunset he made camp on the bank of a clear brook, with grass and wood in abundance—such a campsite as a prospector dreamed of but seldom found.

Before dark Jenet's long ears told of the advent of strangers. A man and a woman rode down the trail into Tappan's camp. They had poor horses and led a pack animal that appeared too old and weak to bear up under even the meager pack he carried.

"Howdy," said the man.

Tappan rose from his task to his lofty height and returned the greeting. The man was middle-aged, swarthy, and rugged, a mountaineer, with something about him that relegated him to the men of the open who Tappan instinctively distrusted. The woman was under thirty, comely in a full-blown way, with rich brown skin and glossy dark hair. She had wide-open black eyes that bent a curious, possession-taking gaze upon Tappan. "Care if we camp with you?" she inquired, and she smiled.

That smile changed Tappan's habit and conviction of a

lifetime. "No, indeed. Reckon I'd like a little company," he said.

Very probably Jenet did not understand Tappan's words, but she dropped one ear, and walked out of camp to the green bank.

"Thanks, stranger," replied the woman. "That grub shore smells good." She hesitated a moment, evidently waiting to catch her companion's eye, then she continued. "My name's Madge Beam. He's my brother Jake. Who might you happen to be?"

"I'm Tappan, lone prospector, as you see," replied Tappan.

"Tappan! What's your front handle?" she queried.

"Fact is, I don't remember," replied Tappan as he brushed a huge hand through his shaggy hair.

"Ahuh? Any name's good enough."

When she dismounted, Tappan saw that she was a tall, lithe figure, garbed in rider's overalls and boots. She unsaddled her horse with a dexterity of long practice. She carried the saddlebags over to the spot Jake had selected to throw the pack.

Tappan heard them talking in low tones. How strange he felt it was that he did not react as usual to an invasion of his privacy and solitude. Tappan had thrilled under those black eyes, and now a queer sensation of the unusual rose in him. Bending over his campfire tasks, he pondered this and that, but mostly the sense of the nearness of a woman. Like most desert men, Tappan knew little of women. He had never felt the necessity of a woman. A few that he might have been drawn to had gone out of his wandering life as quickly as they had entered it. No woman had ever made him feel as this Madge Beam. In evidence of Tappan's preoccupation was the fact that he burned his first batch of biscuits, and Tappan felt proud of his culinary ability. He was on his knees, mixing more flour and water, when the woman spoke from right behind him.

"Tough luck you browned the first pan," she said. "But it's a good turn for your burro. That shore is a burro. Biggest I ever saw." Thereupon she picked up the burned biscuits and tossed them over to Jenet, then she came back to Tappan's side, rather embarrassingly close. "Tappan, I know how I'll eat, so I ought to ask you to let me help," she said with a laugh.

"No, I don't need any," replied Tappan. "You sit down on my roll of beddin' there. Must be tired, aren't you?"

"Not so very," she returned. "That is, I'm not tired of ridin'." She spoke the second part of this reply in a lower tone.

Tappan looked up from his task. The woman had washed her face, brushed her hair, and had put on a skirt—a singularly attractive change. Tappan thought her younger. She was the handsomest woman he had ever seen. The look of her made him clumsy. What eyes she had! They looked through him. Tappan returned to his task, wondering if he was right in his feeling that she wanted to be friendly.

"Jake an' I drove a bunch of cattle to Maricopa," she said. "We sold it, an' Jake gambled away most of the money. I couldn't get what I wanted."

"Too bad. So you're ranchers. Once thought I'd like that. Fact is, down here at Globe a few weeks ago I came near buyin' some rancher out an' tryin' the game."

"You did?" Her query had a low, quick eagerness that somehow thrilled Tappan, but he did not look up. "I'm a wanderer. I'd never do on a ranch."

"But if you had a woman?" Her laugh was subtle and gay.

"A woman! For me? Oh, Lord, no!"

"Why not? Are you a woman hater?"

"I can't say that," replied Tappan soberly. "It's just . . . I guess . . . no woman would have me."

"Faint heart never won fair lady."

Tappan had no reply for that. He surely was making a mess of this second pan of biscuit dough. Manifestly the woman saw this, for, with a laugh, she plumped down on her knees in front of Tappan, and rolled up her sleeves over shapely brown arms.

"Poor man! Shore you need a woman. Let me show you," she said, and put her hands right down upon Tappan's. The touch gave him a strange thrill. He had to pull his hands away, and, as he wiped them with his scarf, he looked at her. He seemed compelled to look. She was close to him now, smiling in good nature, a little scornful of man's encroachment upon the housewifely duties of a woman. A subtle something emanated from her—more than kindness or gaiety. Tappan grasped that it was just the woman of her, and it was going to his head.

"Very well, let's see you show me," he replied as he rose to his feet.

Just then, her brother Jake strolled over, and he had a rather amused and derisive eye for his sister. "Wal, Tappan, she's not over fond of work, but I reckon she can cook," he said.

Tappan felt greatly relieved at the approach of the brother, and he fell into conversation with him, telling something of his prospecting since leaving Globe and listening to the man's cattle talk. By and by the woman called: "Come an' get it!" Then they sat down to eat, and as usual with hungry wayfarers they did not talk much until appetite was satisfied. Afterward, before the campfire, they began to talk again, Jake doing the most of it. Tappan conceived the idea that the rancher was rather curious about him and perhaps wanted to sell his ranch. The woman seemed more thoughtful, with her wide black eyes on the fire.

"Tappan, what way you travelin'?" Beam finally inquired.

"Can't say. I just worked down out of the Superstitions. Haven't any place in mind. Where does this road go?"

"To the Tonto Basin. Ever heard of it?"

"Yes, the name isn't new. What's in this basin?"

The man grunted. "Tonto once was home for the Apaches. It's now got a few sheep an' cattlemen, lots of rustlers. An', say,

59

if you like to hunt bear an' deer, come along with us."

"Thanks. I don't know as I can," returned Tappan irresolutely. He was not used to such possibilities as this suggested.

Then Madge Beam spoke up. "It's a pretty country. Wild an' different. We live up under Mogollon Rim. There's minerals in the cañons."

Was it what was said about minerals that decided Tappan or the look in her eyes?

Tappan's world of thought and feeling underwent as great a change as this Tonto Basin differed from the stark desert so long his home. The trail to the log cabin of the Beams climbed many a ridge and slope and foothill, all covered with manzanita, mescal, cedar, and juniper, at last reaching the cañons of the rim where lofty pines and spruces lorded it over the under forest of maples and oaks. Although the yellow Mogollon Rim towered high over the site of the cabin, the altitude was still great, close to seven thousand feet above sea level.

Tappan had fallen in love with this wild wooded and cañoned country. So had Jenet. It was rather funny the way she hung around Tappan, mornings and evenings. She ate luxuriant grass and oak leaves until her sides bulged.

There did not appear to be any flat places in this country. Every bench was either uphill or downhill. The Beams had no garden or farm or ranch that Tappan could discover. They raised a few acres of sorghum and corn. Their log cabin was of the most primitive kind, and outfitted poorly. Madge Beam explained that this cabin was their winter abode, and that up on the rim they had a good house and ranch. Tappan did not inquire closely into anything. If he had interrogated himself, he would have found out that the reason he did not inquire was because he feared something might remove him from the vicinity of Madge Beam. He had thought it strange the Beams avoided wayfarers they had met on the trail and had gone around a little hamlet Tappan had espied from a hill. Madge Beam, with woman's intuition, had read his mind and had said: "Jake doesn't get along so well with some of the villagers. An' I've no hankerin' for gun play." That explanation was sufficient for Tappan. He had lived long enough in his wandering years to appreciate that people could have reasons for being solitary.

This trip up into the rimrock country bade fairly to become Tappan's one and only adventure of the heart. It was not alone the murmuring clear brook of cold mountain water that enchanted him, nor the stately pines, nor the beautiful silver spruces, nor the wonder of the deep, yellow-walled cañons, so choked with verdure and haunted by wild creatures. He dared not face his soul and ask why this dark-eyed woman sought him more and more, and grew from gay and audacious, even bantering, to sweet and melancholy, and sometimes somber as an Indian. Tappan lived in the moment.

He was aware that the few mountaineer neighbors who rode that way rather avoided contact with him. Tappan was not so dense but he saw that the Beams would rather keep him from outsiders. This was perhaps owing to their desire to sell Tappan the ranch and cattle. Jake offered to sell at what he called a low figure. Tappan thought it just as well to go out into the forest and hide his bags of gold. He did not trust Jake Beam, and liked less the looks of the men who visited this wilderness ranch. Madge Beam might be related to a rustler and be the associate of rustlers, but that did not necessarily make her a bad woman. Tappan guessed that her attitude was changing, and she seemed to require his respect; all she wanted was his admiration. Tappan's long unused deference for a woman returned to him, and he saw that Madge Beam was not used to deference. When Tappan saw that it was having some strong softening effect upon her, he redoubled his attentions. They rode and climbed and hunted together. Tappan had pitched his camp not far from the cabin, on a shaded bank of the singing brook. Madge did not leave him much to himself. She was always coming up to his camp on one pretext or another. Often she would bring two horses and make Tappan ride with her. Some of these occasions, Tappan saw, happened to occur while visitors were at the cabin. In three weeks Madge Beam changed from the bold and careless woman who had ridden down into his camp that sunset to a serious and appealing woman, growing more careful of her person and adornment, and manifestly bearing a burden on her mind.

October came. In the morning white frost glistened on the split-wood shingles of the cabin. The sun soon melted it, and grew warm. The afternoons were still and smoky, melancholy with the enchantment of Indian summer. Tappan hunted wild turkeys and deer with Madge, and revived his boyish love of such pursuits. Madge appeared to be a woman of the woods and had no mean skill with the rifle.

One day they were high on the Mogollon Rim with the great timbered basin at their feet. They had come up to hunt deer, but got no farther than the wonderful promontory where before they had lingered.

"Somethin' will happen to us today," Madge Beam said enigmatically.

Tappan never had been much of a talker, but he could listen. The woman unburdened herself this day. She wanted freedom, happiness, a home away from this lonely country, and all the heritage of woman. She confessed it broodingly, passionately, and Tappan recognized truth when he heard it. He was ready to do all in his power for this woman and believed she knew it, but words and acts of sentiment came hard to him.

"Are you goin' to buy Jake's ranch?" she asked.

"I don't know. Is there any hurry?" returned Tappan.

"I reckon not. But I think I'll settle that," she said decisively.

"How so?"

"Well, Jake hasn't got any ranch," she answered, and added hastily, "no clear title, I mean. He's only homesteaded one hundred an' sixty acres, an' hasn't proved up on it yet. But don't you say I told you."

"Was Jake aimin' to be crooked?"

"I reckon . . . an' I was willin' at first. But not now."

Tappan did not speak at once. He saw the woman was in one of her brooding moods. Besides, he wanted to weigh her words. How significant they were! Today more than ever before she had let down. Humility and simplicity seemed to abide with her, and her brooding boded a storm. Tappan's heart swelled in his broad breast. Was life going to dawn rosy and bright for the lonely prospector? He had money to make a home for this woman. What lay in the balance of the hour? Tappan waited, slowly realizing the charged atmosphere.

Madge's somber eyes gazed out over the great void, but full of thought and passion, as they were, they did not see the beauty of that scene. Tappan saw it, and in some strange sense the color and wildness and sublimity seemed the expression of a new state of his heart. Under him sheered down the ragged and cracked cliffs of the Mogollon Rim, yellow and gold and gray, full of caves and crevices, ledges for eagles and niches for lions, a thousand feet down to the upward edge of the long green slopes and cañons, and so on down and down into the abyss of forested ravine and ridge, rolling league on league away to the encompassing barrier of purple mountain ranges. The thickets in the cañons called Tappan's eye back to linger there. How different from the scenes that had used to be perpetually in his sight! What riot of color! The tips of the green pines, the crests of the silver spruces, waved about masses of vivid gold of aspen trees, and wonderful cerise and flaming red of maples, and

63

Zane Grey

crags of yellow rock covered with the bronze of frost-bitten sumac. Here was autumn and the colors of Tappan's favorite season. From below breathed up the roar of plunging brook; an eagle screeched his wild call; an elk bugled his piercing blast. From the rim wisps of pine needles blew away on the breeze and fell into the void. A wild country, colorful, beautiful, bountiful! Tappan imagined he could quell his wandering spirit here, with this dark-eyed woman by his side. Never before had Nature so called him. Here was not the cruelty of the flinty hardness of the desert. The air was keen and sweet, cold in the shade, warm in the sun. A fragrance of balsam and spruce, spiced with pine, made his breathing a thing of difficulty and delight. How for so many years had he endured vast open spaces without such eye-soothing trees as these? Tappan's back rested against a huge pine that tipped the rim and had stood there, stronger than the storms, for many a hundred years. The rock of the promontory was covered with soft, brown mats of pine needles. A juniper tree, with its bright green foliage and lilac-colored berries, grew near the pine and helped to form a secluded little nook, fragrant and somehow haunting. The woman's dark head was close to Tappan, as she sat with her elbows on her knees, gazing down into the basin. Tappan saw the strained tensity of her posture, the heaving of her full bosom. He wondered, while his own emotions, so long deadened, roused to the suspense of that hour.

Suddenly she flung herself into Tappan's arms. The act amazed him. It seemed to have both the passion of a woman and the shame of a girl. Before she hid her face on Tappan's breast, he saw how the rich brown had paled, and then flamed.

"Tappan . . . ! Take me away . . . take me away from here . . . from that life down there," she cried in smothered voice.

"Madge, you mean take you away . . . and marry you?" he replied.

64

"Oh, yes . . . yes . . . marry me, if you love me. I don't see how you can . . . but you do, don't you? Say you do."

"I reckon that's what ails me, Madge," he replied simply.

"*Say* so, then!" she burst out.

"All right, I do," said Tappan with heavy breath. "Madge, words don't come easy for me . . . but I think you're wonderful, an' I want you. I haven't dared hope for that, till now. I'm only a wanderer. But it'd be heaven to have you . . . my wife . . . an' make a home for you."

"Oh . . . oh!" she returned wildly, and lifted herself to cling around his neck and to kiss him. "You give me joy . . . oh, Tappan, I love you. I never loved any man before. I know now . . . an' I'm not wonderful . . . or good. But I love you."

The fire of her lips and the clasp of her arms worked havoc in Tappan. No woman had ever loved him, let alone embraced him. To awake suddenly to such rapture as this made him strong and rough in his response. Then all at once she seemed to collapse in his arms and began to weep. He feared he had offended or hurt her and was clumsy in his contrition.

Presently she replied. "Pretty soon . . . I'll make you beat me. It's your love . . . your honesty . . . that's shamed me. Tappan, I was party to a trick to . . . sell you a worthless ranch. I agreed to . . . try to make you love me . . . to fool you . . . cheat you. But I've fallen in love with you, an', my God, I care more for your love . . . your respect . . . than for my life. I can't go on with it. I've double-crossed Jake, an' all of them. Dear, am I worth lovin'? Am I worth havin'?"

"More than ever, dear," he said.

"You will take me away?"

"Anywhere . . . anytime, the sooner the better."

She kissed him passionately, and then, dislodging herself from his arms, she kneeled and gazed earnestly at him. "I've not told all. I will someday. But I swear now on my very soul . . . I'll

65

be what you think me."

"Madge, you needn't say all that. If you love me . . . it's enough. More than I ever dreamed of."

"You're a man. Oh, why didn't I meet you when I was eighteen instead of now . . . twenty-eight, an' all that between. But enough. A new life begins here for us. We must plan."

"You make the plans, an' I'll act on them."

For a moment she was tense and silent, head lowered, hands shut tightly. Then she spoke. "Tonight we'll slip away. You make a light pack that'll go on your saddle. I'll do the same. We'll run off . . . ride out of the country."

Tappan tried to think, but the swirl of his mind made any reasoning difficult. This dark-eyed, full-bosomed woman loved him, had surrendered herself, asked only his protection. The thing seemed marvelous. She kneeled there, those dark eyes on him, infinitely more appealing than ever, haunting with some mystery of sadness and fear he could not divine.

Suddenly Tappan remembered Jenet. "I must take Jenet," he said.

That startled her. "Jenet . . . who's she?"

"My burro."

"Your burro. You can't travel fast with that pack beast. We'll be trailed, an' we'll have to go fast. You can't take the burro."

Then Tappan was startled. "What! Can't take Jenet? Why, I . . . I couldn't get along without her."

"Nonsense. What's a burro? We must ride fast . . . do you hear?"

"Madge, I'm afraid I . . . I must take Jenet with me," he said soberly.

"It's impossible. I can't go if you take her. I tell you, I've got to get away. If you want me, you'll have to leave your precious Jenet behind."

Tappan bowed his head to the inevitable. After all, Jenet was only a beast of burden. She would run wild on the ridges and soon forget him and have no need of him. Something strained in Tappan's breast. He had to see clearly here. This woman was worth more than all else to him. "I'm stupid, dear," he said. "You see I never before ran off with a beautiful woman. Of course, my burro must be left behind."

Elopement, if such it could be called, was easy for them. Tappan did not understand why Madge wanted to be so secret about it. Was she not free? But then he reflected that he did not know the circumstances she feared. Besides, he did not care. Possession of the woman was enough.

Tappan made his small pack, the weight of which was considerable owing to his bags of gold. This he tied on his saddle. It bothered him to leave most of his new outfit scattered around his camp. What would Jenet think of that? He looked for her, but for once she did not come in at mealtime. Tappan thought this was singular. He could not remember when Jenet had been far from his camp at sunset. Somehow Tappan was glad.

After he had his supper, he left his utensils and supplies as they happened to be and strode away under the trees to the trysting-place where he was to meet Madge. To his surprise she came before dark, and, unused as he was to the complexity and emotional nature of a woman, he saw that she was strangely agitated. Her face was pale. Almost a fury burned in her black eyes. When she came up to Tappan and embraced him almost fiercely, he felt that he was about to learn more of the nature of womankind. She thrilled him to his depths.

"Lead out the horses an' don't make any noise," she whispered.

Tappan complied, and soon he was mounted, riding behind her on the trail. It surprised him that she headed downcountry and traveled fast. Moreover, she kept to a trail that continually grew rougher. They came to a road, which she crossed, and kept on through darkness and brush so thick that Tappan could not see the least sign of a trail. At length, anyone could have seen that Madge had lost her bearings. She appeared to know the direction she wanted, but traveling upon it was impossible owing to the increasingly cut-up and brushy ground. They had to turn back and seemed to be hours finding the road. Once Tappan fancied he heard the thud of hoofs other than those made by their own horses. Here Madge acted strangely, and, where she had been obsessed by a desire to hurry, she now seemed to have grown weary. She turned her horse south on the road. Tappan was thus able to ride beside her, but they talked very little. He was satisfied with the fact of being with her on the way out of the country. Woman-like perhaps, she had begun to feel the pangs of remorse. Sometime in the night they reached an old log shack by the side of the road. Here Tappan suggested they halt, and get some sleep before dawn. The morrow would mean a long hard day.

"Yes, tomorrow will be hard," replied Madge, as she faced Tappan in the gloom. He could see her big dark eyes on him. Her tone was not one of a hopeful woman. Tappan pondered over this, but he could not understand because he had no idea how a woman ought to act under such circumstances. Madge Beam was a creature of moods. Only the day before, on the ride down from the rim, she had told him with a laugh that she was likely to love him madly one moment and scratch his eyes out the next. How could he know what to make of her? Still, an uneasy feeling began to stir in Tappan.

They dismounted and unsaddled the horses. Tappan took his pack and put it inside. Something frightened the horses. They bolted down the road.

"Head them off," cried the woman hoarsely.

Even on the instant her voice sounded strained to Tappan, as if she were choked, but, realizing the absolute necessity of catching the horses, he set off down the road on a run. He soon succeeded in heading off the horse he had ridden. The other one, however, was contrary and cunning. When Tappan would endeavor to get ahead of it, it would trot briskly on. Yet it did not go so fast but what Tappan felt sure he would soon catch it. Thus, walking and running, he got quite a long distance from the cabin before he realized that he could not head off this wary horse. Much perturbed in mind Tappan hurried back.

Upon reaching the cabin, Tappan called to Madge. No answer! He could not see her in the gloom or the horse he had driven back. Only silence brooded there. Tappan called again. Still no answer! Perhaps Madge had succumbed to the weariness and was asleep. A search of the cabin and the vicinity failed to yield any sign of her, but it disclosed the fact that Tappan's pack was gone.

Suddenly he sat down, quite overcome. He had been duped. What a fierce pang tore his heart. But it was for loss of the woman—not the gold. He was stunned and sick with bitter misery. Only then did Tappan realize the meaning of love and what it had done to him. The night wore on, and he sat there in the dark and cold and stillness until the gray dawn told him of the coming of day.

The light showed his saddle lying where he had left it. Nearby lay one of Madge's gloves. Tappan's keen eye sighted a bit of paper sticking out of the glove. He picked it up. It was a leaf out of a little book he had seen her carry, and upon it was written in lead pencil:

I am Jake's wife, not his sister. I double-crossed him and ran off with you and would have gone to hell for you. But Jake and his gang suspected me. They were close on our tail. I couldn't

shake them. So here I chased off the horses and sent you after
them. It was the only way I could save your life.

Tappan tracked the thieves to Globe. There he learned they had
gone to Phoenix—three men and one woman. Tappan had
money on his person. He bought horse and saddle, and, setting
out for Phoenix, he let his passion to kill grow with the miles
and hours. At Phoenix he learned Beam had cashed the gold—
$12,000. So much of a fortune! Tappan's fury grew. The gang
separated here. Beam and his wife took the stage for Tucson.
Tappan had his trouble in trailing their movements. Gambling
dives and inns and freighting posts and stage drivers told the
story of the Beams and their ill-gotten gold. They went on down
into Tappan's country, to Yuma and El Cajon, and then San
Diego in California. Here Tappan lost track of the woman. He
could not find that she had left San Diego, nor any trace of her
there. But Jake Beam had killed a Mexican in a brawl and had
fled across the line.

Tappan gave up the chase of Beam for the time being and
lent his efforts to finding the woman. He had no resentment
toward Madge. He only loved her. All that winter he searched
San Diego. He made of himself a peddler as a ruse to visit
houses, but he never found a trace of her. In the spring he
wandered back to Yuma, raking over the old clues, and so on
back to Tucson and Phoenix.

This year of dream and love and passion and despair and
hate made Tappan old. His great strength and endurance were
not yet impaired, but something wonderful died out of him.
One day he remembered Jenet. "My burro," he soliloquized. "I
had forgotten her . . . Jenet!"

Then it seemed a thousand impulses merged into one and
drove him to face the long road toward the rimrock country. To
remember Jenet was to grow doubtful. Of course, she would be

gone. Stolen or dead or wandered off. But then, who could tell what Jenet might do? Tappan was both called and driven. He was a poor wanderer again. His outfit was a pack he carried on his shoulder. But while he could walk, he would keep on until he reached that last camp where he had deserted Jenet.

October was coloring the cañon slopes when he reached the shadow of the great wall of yellow rock. There was no cabin where the Beams had lived—or claimed they lived—or a fallen ruin, crushed by snow. Tappan saw the signs of a severe winter and heavy snowfall. No horse or cattle tracks showed on the trails.

To his amazement, his camp was much as he had left it. The stove fireplace, the iron pots appeared to be where he had left them. The boxes that had held his supplies were lying here and there, and his canvas tarpaulin, little the worse for wear or the elements, lay on the ground under the pine where he had slept. If any man had visited this camp in a year, he had left no sign of it.

Suddenly Tappan espied a hoof track in the dust. A small track—almost oval in shape—fresh! Tappan thrilled through all his being. "Jenet's track, so help me God," he murmured.

He found more of them, made that morning, and, keen now as never before on her trail, he set out to find her. The tracks led up the cañon. Tappan came out into a little grassy clearing, and there stood Jenet as he had seen her thousands of times. She had both long ears up high. She seemed to stare out of that meek, gray face, and then one of the long ears flopped over and drooped. Such perhaps was the expression of her recognition.

Tappan strode up to her. "Jenet . . . old girl . . . you hung 'round camp . . . waitin' for me, didn't you?" he said huskily, and his big hands fondled her long ears.

Yes, she had waited. She, too, had grown old. She was gray. The winter had been hard. What had she lived on when the snow lay so deep? There were lion scratches on her back and scars on her legs. She had fought for her life.

"Jenet, a man can never always tell about a burro," said Tappan. "I trained you to hang 'round camp an' wait till I came back. Tappan's burro, the desert rats used to say. An' they'd laugh when I bragged how you'd stick to me where most men would quit. But brag as I did, I never knew you, Jenet. An' I left you . . . an' forgot. Jenet, it takes a human bein' . . . a man . . . a woman . . . to be faithless. An' it takes a dog or a horse or a burro to be great. Beasts? I wonder now. . . . Well, old pard, we're goin' down the trail together, an' from this day on Tappan begins to pay his debt."

III

Tappan never again had the old wanderlust for the stark and naked desert. Something had transformed him. The green and fragrant forests and brown-aisled, pine-matted woodlands, the craggy promontories and the great colored cañons, the cold-granite water springs of the Tonto seemed vastly preferable to the heat and dust and glare and the emptiness of the wastelands. But there was more. The ghost of his strange and only love kept pace with his wandering steps, a spirit that hovered with him as his shadow. Madge Beam, whatever she had been, had showed to him the power of love to refine and ennoble. Somehow he felt closer to her here in the cliff country where his passion had been born. Somehow she seemed nearer to him here than in all those places he had tracked her.

So, from a prospector searching for gold, Tappan became a hunter seeking only the means to keep soul and body together. All he cared for was his faithful burro Jenet, and the loneliness and silence of the forestland. He learned that the Tonto was a hard country in many ways, and bitterly so in winter. Down in the breaks of the basin it was mild in winter, the snow did not lay long, and ice seldom formed. But up on the rim, where Tappan always lingered as long as possible, the storm king of the north held full sway. Fifteen feet of snow and zero weather was the rule in dead of winter.

An old native once said to Tappan: "See hyar, friend, I reckon you'd better not get caught up in the rimrock country in one of our big storms. Fer if you do, you'll never get out."

It was a way of Tappan's to follow his inclinations, regardless of advice. He had weathered the terrible midnight storm of hot wind in Death Valley. What were snow and cold to him? Late autumn on the Mogollon Rim was the most perfect and beautiful of seasons. He had seen the forestland brown and darkly green one day, and the next burdened with white snow. What a transfiguration! Then, when the sun loosened the white mantling on the pines, and they had shed their burdens in drifting dust of white and rainbowed mists of melting snow, and the avalanches sliding off the branches, there would be left only the wonderful white floor of the woodland. The great rugged brown tree trunks appeared mightier and statelier in the contrast, and the green of foliage, the russet of oak leaves, the gold of the aspens turned the forest into a world enchanting to the desert-scarred eyes of this wanderer of the wasteland.

With Tappan the years sped by. His mind grew old faster than his body. Every season saw him lonelier. He had a feeling, a vague illusive thing, that instead of his bones bleaching on the desert sands, they would mingle with the pine mats and the soft fragrant moss of the forest. The idea was pleasant to Tappan.

One afternoon he was camped in Pine Cañon, a timber-sloped gorge far back from the rim. November was well on. The fall had been singularly open and fair, with not a single storm. A few natives happening across Tappan had remarked casually that such falls sometimes were not to be trusted.

This late afternoon was one of Indian summer beauty and

warmth. The blue haze in the cañon was not just the blue smoke from Tappan's campfire. In a narrow park of grass not far from camp, Jenet grazed peacefully with elk and deer. Tappan never heard the sound of a rifle shot. Wild turkeys lingered there, to seek their winter quarters down in the basin. Gray squirrels and red squirrels barked and frisked, and dropped the pine and spruce cones, with thud and thump, on all the slopes.

Before dark a stranger strode into Tappan's camp, a big man, of middle age, whose magnificent physique impressed even Tappan. He was a rugged, bearded giant, wide-eyed and of pleasant face. He had no outfit, no horse, not even a gun.

"Lucky for me I smelled your smoke," he said. "Two days for me without grub."

"Howdy, stranger," was Tappan's greeting. "Are you lost?"

"Yes an' no. I could find my way out down over the Mogollon Rim, but it's not healthy down there for me. So I'm hittin' north."

"Where's your horse and pack?"

"I reckon they're with the gang that took more of a fancy to them than me."

"Ahuh . . . you're welcome here, stranger," replied Tappan. "I'm Tappan."

"Ha! Heard of you. I'm Jess Blade, of anywhere. An' I'll say I was an honest man till I hit the Tonto."

His laugh was frank for all its note of grimness. Tappan liked the man and sensed one who would be a good friend and bad foe.

"Come an' eat. My supplies are peterin' out, but there's plenty of meat."

Blade ate, indeed as a man starved, and did not seem to care if Tappan's supplies were low. He did not talk. After the meal, he craved a pipe and tobacco. Then he smoked in silence, in slow-realizing content. The morrow had no fears for him. The flickering, ruddy light from the campfire shown on his strong face. Tappan saw in him the drifter, the drinker, the brawler, a man with good in him, but over whom evil passion or temper dominated. Presently he smoked the pipe out, and with reluctant hand knocked out the ashes and returned it to Tappan.

"I reckon I've some news thet'd interest you," he said.

"You have?" queried Tappan.

"Yes, if you're the Tappan who tried to run off with Jake Beam's wife."

"Well, I'm that Tappan. But I'd like to say I didn't know she was married."

"Shore. I remember. So does everybody in the Tonto. You were just meat for thet Beam gang. They had played the trick before. But accordin' to what I hear, thet trick was the last fer Madge Beam. She never came back to this country. An' Jake Beam, when he was drunk, owned up thet she'd left him in California. Some hint at worse. Fer Jake Beam came back a harder man. Even his gang said thet."

"Is he in the Tonto now?" queried Tappan, with a thrill of fire along his veins.

"Yep, thar fer keeps," replied Blade grimly. "Somebody shot him."

"Ahuh!" exclaimed Tappan with a deep breath of relief. There came a sudden check to the heat of his blood.

After that, there was a long silence. Tappan dreamed of the woman who had loved him. Blade brooded over the campfire. The wind moaned fitfully in the lofty pines on the slope. A wolf mourned as if in hunger. The stars appeared to obscure their radiance in haze.

"Reckon thet wind sounds like storm," observed Blade presently.

"I've heard it for weeks now," replied Tappan.

"Are you a woodsman?"

"No, I'm a desert man."

"Wal, you take my hunch and hit the trail fer low country."

This was well-meant and probably sound advice, but it alienated Tappan. He had really liked this hearty-voiced stranger. Tappan thought moodily of his slowly in-growing mind, of the narrowness of his soul. He was past interest in his fellow men. He lived with a dream. The only living creature he loved was a lop-eared lazy burro, growing old in contentment. Nevertheless, that night Tappan shared one of his two blankets.

In the morning the gray dawn broke, and the sun rose without its brightness of gold. There was a haze over the blue sky. Thin, swift-moving clouds scudded up out of the southwest. The wind was chilled, the forest shaggy and dark, the birds and squirrels were silent.

"Wal, you'll break camp today," asserted Blade.

"Nope. I'll stick it out yet a while," returned Tappan.

"But, man, you might get snowed in, an' up hyar thet's serious."

"Ahuh. Well, it won't bother me, an' there's nothin' holdin' you."

"Tappan, it's four days' walk down out of this woods. If a big snow set in, how'd I make it?"

"Then you'd better go out over the rim," suggested Tappan.

"No. I'll take my chance the other way. But are you meanin' you'd rather not have me with you? Fer you can't stay hyar."

Tappan was in a quandary. Some instinct bade him tell the man to go, not empty-handed, but to go. But this was selfish and entirely unlike Tappan, as he remembered himself of old. Finally he spoke. "You're welcome to half my outfit . . . go or stay."

"Thet's mighty square of you, Tappan," responded the other feelingly. "Have you a burro you'll give me?"

"No, I've only one."

"Ha! Then I'll have to stick with you till you leave."

No more was said. They had breakfast in a strange silence. The wind brooded its secret in the treetops. Tappan's burro strolled into camp and caught the stranger's eye.

"Wal, thet's shore a fine burro," he observed. "Never seen the like."

Tappan performed his camp tasks. Then there was nothing to do but sit around the fire. Blade evidently waited for the increasing menace of the storm to rouse Tappan to decision, but the graying over of sky and the increase of wind did not affect Tappan. What did he wait for? The truth of his thoughts was that he did not like the way Jenet remained in camp. She was waiting to be packed. She knew they ought to go. Tappan yielded to a perverse devil of stubbornness. The wind brought a cold mist, then a flurry of wet snow. Tappan gathered firewood, a large quantity. Blade saw this and gave voice to earnest fears, but Tappan paid no heed. By nightfall, sleet and snow began to fall steadily. The men fashioned a rude shack of spruce boughs, ate their supper, and went to bed early.

It worried Tappan that Jenet stayed right in camp. He lay awake a long time. The wind rose and moaned through the forest. The sleet failed, and a soft steady downfall of snow gradually set in. Tappan fell asleep. When he awoke, it was to see a forest of white. The trees were mantled with blankets of wet snow—the ground covered two feet on a level. The clouds appeared to be gone, the sky was blue, the storm over. The sun came up warm and bright.

"It'll all go in a day," said Tappan.

"If this was early October, I'd agree with you," replied Blade. "But it's only makin' fer another storm. Can't you hear thet wind?"

Tappan only heard the whispers of his dream. By noon the

snow was melting off the pines, and rainbows shone everywhere. Little patches of snow began to drop off the south branches of the pines and spruces, and then larger patches, until by midafternoon white streams and avalanches were falling everywhere. All of the snow, except in shaded places on the north sides of trees, went that day, and half of that on the ground. Next day it thinned out more, until Jenet was finding the grass and moss again. That afternoon the telltale thin clouds raced up out of the southwest, and the wind moaned its menace.

"Tappan, let's pack an' hit it out of hyar," appealed Blade anxiously. "I know this country. Mebbe I'm wrong, of course, but it feels like storm. Winter's comin' shore."

"Let her come," replied Tappan imperturbably.

"Say, do you want to get snowed in?" demanded Blade, out of patience.

"I might like a little spell of it, seein' it'd be new to me," replied Tappan.

"But, man, if you ever get snowed in hyar, you can't get out."

"That burro of mine could get me out."

"You're crazy. Thet burro couldn't go a hundred feet. What's more, you'd have to kill her an' eat her."

Tappan bent a strange gaze upon his companion, but made no reply. Blade began to pace up and down the small bare patch of ground before the campfire. Manifestly he was in a serious predicament. That day he seemed subtly to change, as did Tappan. Both answered to their peculiar instincts, Blade to that of self-preservation, and Tappan to something like indifference. Tappan held fate in defiance. What more could happen to him?

Blade broke out again, in eloquent persuasion, giving proof of their peril, and from that he passed to amaze, and then to strident anger. He cursed Tappan for a Nature-loving idiot. "An' I'll tell you what," he ended. "When mornin' comes, I'll take some of your grub an' hit it out of hyar, storm or no storm."

But long before dawn broke that resolution of Blade's became impracticable. Both were awakened by the roar of a storm through the forest, no longer a moan, but a marching roar with now a crash, and then a shriek of gale. By the light of the smoldering campfire Tappan saw a whirling pall of snow, great flakes as large as feathers. Morning disclosed the setting in of a fierce mountain storm, with two feet of snow already on the ground, and the forest lost in a blur of white.

"I was wrong!" called Tappan to his companion. "What's best to do now?"

"You damned fool!" yelled Blade. "We've got to keep from freezin' an' starvin' till the storm ends an' a crust comes on the snow."

For three days and three nights the blizzard continued, unabated in its fury. It took the men hours to keep a space cleared for their campsite, which Jenet shared with them. On the fourth day the storm ceased, the clouds broke away, the sun came out, and the temperature dropped to zero. Snow on the level just topped Tappan's lofty stature, and in drifts it was ten and fifteen feet deep. Winter had set in with a vengeance. The forest became a solemn, still, white world. But now Tappan had no time to dream. Dry firewood was hard to find under the snow. It was possible to cut down one of the dead trees on the slope, but impossible to pack sufficient wood to the camp. They had to burn green wood. Then the fashioning of snowshoes took much time. Tappan had no knowledge of such footgear. He could only help Blade. The men were encouraged by the piercing cold forming a crust on the snow. But just as they were about to pack and venture forth, the weather moderated, the crust refused to hold their weight, and another foot of snow fell.

"Why in hell didn't you kill an elk?" demanded Blade sullenly. He had changed from friendly to darkly sinister. He knew the peril, and he loved life. "Now we'll have to kill an' eat your precious Jenet. An' mebbe she won't furnish meat enough to last till this snow weather stops an' a good freeze'll make travelin' possible."

"Blade, you shut up about killin' an' eatin' my burro Jenet," returned Tappan in a voice that silenced the other.

Thus instinctively these men became enemies. Blade thought only of himself. For himself Tappan had not one thought. Tappan's supplies ran low. All the bacon and coffee were gone. There was only a small haunch of venison, a bag of beans, a sack of flour, and a small quantity of salt left.

"If a crust freezes on the snow an' we can pack thet flour, we'll get out alive," said Blade. "But we can't take the burro."

Another day of bright sunshine softened the snow on the southern exposures, and a night of piercing cold froze a crust that would bear the quick step of a man.

"It's our only chance . . . an' damned slim at thet," declared Blade.

Tappan allowed Blade to choose the time and method and supplies for the start to get out of the forest. They cooked all the beans and divided them in two sacks. Then they baked about four pounds of biscuits for each of them. Blade showed his cunning when he chose the small bag of salt for himself and let Tappan take the tobacco. This quantity of food and a blanket for each, Blade declared, was all they could pack. They argued over the guns, and in the end Blade compromised on the rifle, agreeing to let Tappan carry that on the possible chance of killing a deer or elk. When this matter had been decided, Blade significantly began putting on his rude snowshoes that had been constructed from pieces of Tappan's boxes and straps and burlap sacks.

"Reckon they won't last long," muttered Blade.

Meanwhile, Tappan fed Jenet some biscuits, and then began to strap a tarpaulin on her back.

"What ya doin?" queried Blade suddenly.

"Gettin' Jenet ready," replied Tappan.

"Ready . . . fer what?"

"Why, to go with us."

"Hell!" shouted Blade, and he threw up his hands in helpless rage.

Tappan felt a depth stirred within him. He lost his late taciturnity and his silent aloofness fell away from him. Blade seemed on the moment no longer an enemy. He loomed as an aid to the saving of Jenet. Tappan burst into speech. "I can't go without her. It'd never enter my head. Jenet's mother was a good faithful burro. I saw Jenet born way down there on the Río Colorado. She wasn't strong, an' I had to wait for her to be able to walk. She grew up. Her mother died, an' Jenet an' me packed it alone. She wasn't no ordinary burro. She learned all I taught her. She was different. But I treated her same as any burro, an' she grew with the years. Desert men said there never was such a burro as Jenet. Called her Tappan's burro, an' tried to borrow an' buy an' steal her. How many times in ten years Jenet has done me a good turn I can't remember. But she saved my life. She dragged me out of Death Valley. An' then I forgot my debt. I ran off with a woman an' left Jenet to wait as she had been trained to wait. I knew she'd wait at that camp till I came back. She'd have starved there! Well, I got back in time . . . an' now I'll not leave her here. It may be strange to you, Blade, me carin' this way. Jenet's only a burro. But I won't leave her."

"Man, you talk like thet lazy lop-eared burro was a woman," declared Blade in disgusted astonishment.

"I don't know women, but I reckon Jenet's more faithful than most of them."

"Wal, of all the stark starin' fools I ever run into, you're the worst."

"Fool or not, I know what I'll do," retorted Tappan. The softer mood left him swiftly.

"Haven't you sense enough to see thet we can't travel with your burro?" queried Blade, patiently controlling his temper. "She has little hoofs, sharp as knives. She'll cut through the crust. She'll break through in places, an' we'll have to stop to haul her out . . . mebbe break through ourselves. That would make us longer gettin' out."

"Long or short, we'll take her."

Then Blade confronted Tappan as if suddenly unmasking his true meaning. His patient explanation meant nothing. Under no circumstances would he ever have consented to an attempt to take Jenet out of that snow-bound wilderness. His eyes gleamed. "We've a hard pull to get out alive. An' hard-workin' men in winter must have meat to eat."

Tappan slowly straightened up to look at the speaker. "What do you mean?"

For answer, Blade jerked his hand backward and downward, and, when it swung into sight again, it held Tappan's worn and shining rifle. Blade, with deliberate force that showed the nature of the man, worked the lever and threw a shell into the magazine, all the while his eyes fastened on Tappan. His face seemed that of another man, evil, relentless, inevitable in his spirit to preserve his own life at any cost. "I mean to kill your burro," he said in voice that suited his look and manner.

"No!" cried Tappan, shocked into an instant of appeal.

"Yes, I am, an' I'll bet, by God, before we get out of hyar you'll be glad to eat some of her meat!"

That roused the slow-gathering might of Tappan's wrath. "I'd starve to death before I'd . . . I'd kill that burro, let alone eat her."

"Starve and be damned!" shouted Blade, yielding to rage.

Jenet stood right behind Tappan, in her posture of contented repose, with one long ear hanging down over her gray, meek face.

"You'll have to kill me first," answered Tappan sharply.

"I'm good fer anythin' . . . if you push me," returned Blade stridently.

As he stepped aside, evidently so he could have unobstructed aim at Jenet, Tappan leaped forward and knocked up the rifle as it was discharged. The bullet sped harmlessly over Jenet. Tappan heard it thud into a tree. Blade uttered a curse. As he lowered the rifle, in sudden deadly intent Tappan grasped the barrel with his left hand. Then, clenching his right, he struck Blade a sudden blow in the face. Only Blade's hold on the rifle prevented him from falling. Blood streamed from his nose and mouth. He bellowed in hoarse fury: "I'll kill you fer thet!"

Tappan opened his clenched teeth. "No, Blade . . . you're not man enough."

Then began a terrific struggle for possession of the rifle. Tappan beat at Blade's face with his sledge-hammer fist, and the strength of the other made it imperative that Blade use both hands to keep his hold on the rifle. Wrestling and pulling and jerking, the men tore around the snowy camp, scattering the campfire, knocking down the brush shelter. Blade had surrendered to a wild frenzy. He hissed his maledictions. His was the brute lust to kill an enemy that thwarted him. But Tappan was grim and terrible in his restraint. His battle was to save Jenet. Nevertheless, there mounted in him the hot physical sensations of the savage. The contact of flesh, the smell and sight of Blade's blood, the violent action, the beastly mien of his foe changed the fight to one for its own sake. To conquer this foe, to rend him and beat him down, blow on blow!

Tappan felt instinctively that he was the stronger. Suddenly he exerted all his muscular force into one tremendous wrench. The rifle broke, leaving the steel barrel in his hands, the wooden stock in Blade's. It was the quicker-witted Blade who used his weapon first to advantage. One swift blow knocked down Tappan. As he was about to follow it up with another, Tappan kicked his opponent's feet from under him. Blade sprawled in the snow, but was up again as quickly as Tappan. They made at each other, Tappan waiting to strike, and Blade raining blows aimed at his head, but which Tappan contrived to receive on his arms and the rifle barrel he brandished. For a few minutes Tappan stood up under a beating that would have felled a lesser man. His own blood blinded him. Then he swung his heavy weapon. The blow broke Blade's left arm. Like a wild beast he screamed in pain, and then, without guard, rushed in, too furious for further caution. Tappan met the terrible onslaught as before and, snatching his chance, again swung the rifle barrel. This time, so supreme was the force, it battered down Blade's arm and crushed his skull. He died on his feet—ghastly and horrible change!—and, swaying backward, he fell into the banked wall of snow and went out of sight, except for his boots, one of which still held the crude snowshoe.

Tappan stared, slowly realizing.

"Ahuh, stranger Blade!" he ejaculated, gazing at the hole in the snowbank where his foe had disappeared. "You were goin' to kill an' eat . . . Tappan's burro!"

Then he sighted the bloody rifle barrel, and cast it from him. It appeared then that he had sustained injuries that needed attention, but he could do little more than wash off the blood and bind up his head. Both arms and hands were badly bruised and beginning to swell. Fortunately no bones had been broken.

Tappan finished strapping the tarpaulin upon the burro, and, taking up both his and Blade's supply of food, he called out: "Come on, Jenet!"

Which way to go? Indeed, there was no more choice for him

than there had been for Blade. Toward the Mogollon Rim the snowdrift would be deeper, and impassable. Tappan realized that the only possible chance for him was downhill. So he led Jenet out of camp without looking back once. What was it that had happened? He did not seem to be the same Tappan that had dreamily tramped into this woodland.

A deep furrow in the snow had been made by the men packing firewood into their camp. At the end of this furrow the wall of snow stood up higher than Tappan's head. To get out on top without breaking the crust presented a problem. He lifted Jenet up and was relieved to see that the snow held her, but he found a different task in his own case. Returning to camp, he gathered up several of the long branches of spruce that had been part of the shelter, and, carrying them out, he laid them against the slant of snow he had to surmount, and by their aid he got on top. The crust held him.

Elated and with revived hope, he took up Jenet's halter and started off. Walking with his rude snowshoes was awkward. He had to go slowly and slide them along the crust. But he progressed. Jenet's little steps kept her even with him. Now and then one of her sharp hoofs cut through, but not to hinder her particularly. Right at the start Tappan observed something singular about Jenet. Never until now had she been dependent upon him. She knew it. Her intelligence apparently told her that, if she got out of this snow-bound wilderness, it would be owing to the strength and reason of her master.

Tappan kept to the north side of the cañon where the snow crust was strongest. What he must do was to work up to the top of the cañon slope, and then keep to the ridge, travel north along it, and so down out of the forest. Travel was slow. He soon found he had to pick his way. Jenet appeared to be absolutely unable to sense either danger or safety. Her experience had been of the rock confines and the drifting sands of the

85

desert. She walked where Tappan led her, and it seemed to Tappan that her trust in him, her reliance upon him, were pathetic.

"Well, old girl," said Tappan, "it's a horse of another color now . . . hey?"

At length he came to a wide part of the cañon, where a bench of land led to a long gradual slope, thickly studded with small pines. This appeared to be fortunate and turned out to be so, for, when Jenet broke through the crust, Tappan had trees and branches to hold while he hauled her out. The labor of climbing that slope was such that Tappan began to appreciate Blade's absolute refusal to attempt getting Jenet out. Dusk was shadowing the white aisles of the forest when Tappan ascended to a level. Yet he had not traveled far from camp, and that fact struck a chill upon his heart.

To go on in the dark was foolhardy. So Tappan selected a thick spruce, under which there was a considerable depression in the snow, and here made preparation to spend the night. Unstrapping the tarpaulin, he spread it on the snow. All the lower branches of this giant of the forest were dead and dry. Tappan broke off many and soon had a fire. Jenet nibbled at the moss on the trunk of the spruce tree. Tappan's meal consisted of beans, biscuits, and a ball of snow that he held over the fire to soften. He saw to it that Jenet fared as well as he. Night soon fell, strange and weirdly white in the forest, and piercingly cold. Tappan needed the fire. Gradually it melted the snow and made a hole down to the ground. Tappan rolled up in the tarpaulin and soon fell asleep.

In three days Tappan traveled about fifteen miles, gradually descending, until the snow crust began to fail to hold Jenet. Then whatever had been his tasks before, they were now magnified. As soon as the sun was up, somewhat softening the snow, Jenet began to break through, and often, when Tappan began hauling her out, he broke through himself. This exertion was killing even to a man of Tappan's physical prowess. Besides the endurance to resist heat and flying dust and dragging sand seemed another kind than that so needed to toil on in this snow. The endless snow-bound forest began to be hideous to Tappan—cold, lonely, dreary, white, mournful, the kind of ghastly and ghostly winter land that had been the terror of Tappan's boyish dreams! He loved the sun, the open. This forest had deceived him. It was a wall of ice. As he toiled on, the state of his mind gradually and subtly changed in all except the fixed and absolute will to save Jenet. In some places he carried her.

The fourth night found him dangerously near the end of his stock of food. He had been generous with Jenet. But now, considering that he had to do more work than she, he diminished her share. On the fifth day Jenet broke through the snow crust so often that Tappan realized how utterly impossible it was for her to get out of the woods by her own efforts. Therefore, Tappan hit upon the plan of making her lie in the tarpaulin, so that he could drag her. The tarpaulin doubled once did not make a bad sled. All the rest of that day Tappan hauled her. And so all the rest of the next day he toiled on, hands behind him, clutching the canvas, head and shoulders bent, plodding and methodical, like a man who could not be defeated. That night he was too weary to build a fire, and too worried to eat the last of his food.

Next day Tappan was not dead to the changing character of the forest. He had worked down out of the zone of the spruce trees; the pines had thinned out and decreased in size; oak trees began to show prominently. All these signs meant that he was getting down out of the mountain heights. But the fact, hopeful as it was, had drawbacks. The snow was still four feet deep on a level, and the crust held Tappan only about half the time. Moreover, the lay of the land operated against Tappan's

progress. The long, slowly descending ridge had failed. There
were no more cañons, but ravines and swales were numerous.
Tappan dragged on, stern, indomitable, bent to his toil.

When the crust no longer held him, he hung his snowshoes
over Jenet's back and wallowed through, making a lane for her
to follow. Two days of such heart-breaking toil, without food or
fire, broke Tappan's magnificent endurance. But not his spirit.
He hauled Jenet over the snow and through the snow, down the
hills and up the slopes, through the thickets, knowing that over
the next ridge perhaps was deliverance. Deer and elk tracks
began to be numerous. Cedar and juniper trees now predomi-
nated. An occasional pine showed here and there. He was getting out of the forestland. Only such mighty hope as that justi-
fied could have kept him on his feet.

He fell often, and it grew harder to rise and go on. The hour
came when he had to abandon hauling Jenet. It was necessary
to make a road for her. How weary, cold, horrible the white
reaches! Yard by yard Tappan made his way. He no longer
perspired. He had no feeling in his feet or legs. Hunger ceased
to gnaw at his vitals. His thirst he quenched with snow—soft
snow now, that did not have to be crunched like ice. The pangs
in his breast were terrible, cramps, constrictions, the piercing
pain in his lungs, the dull ache of his over-taxed heart.

Tappan came to an opening in the cedar forest from which
he could see afar. A long slope fronted him. It led down and
down to the open country. His desert eyes, keen as those of an
eagle, made out flat country, sparsely covered with snow, and
black dots that were cattle. The last slope! The last pull! Three
feet of snow, except in drifts, down and down he plunged, making way for Jenet! All that day he toiled and fell and rolled down
this league-long slope, wearying toward sunset to the end of his
task, and likewise to the end of his will.

Now he seemed up and now down. There was no sense of

cold or weariness, only direction. Tappan still saw! The last of his horror at the monotony of white faded from his mind. Jenet was there, beginning to be able to travel for herself. The solemn close of an endless day found Tappan arriving at the edge of the timbered country where wind-bared patches of ground showed long, bleached grass. Jenet took to grazing.

As for Tappan, he fell with the tarpaulin under a thick cedar, and with strengthless hands plucked and plucked at the canvas to spread it, so that he could cover himself. He looked again for Jenet. She was there, somehow a fading image, strangely blurred. But she was grazing. Tappan lay down and stretched out, and slowly drew the tarpaulin over him.

A piercing cold night wind swept down from the snowy heights. It wailed in the edge of the cedars and moaned out toward the open country. Yet the night seemed silent. The stars shone white in a deep blue sky, passionless, cold, watchful eyes, looking down without pity or hope or censure. They were the eyes of Nature. Winter had locked the heights in its snowy grip. All night that winter wind blew down, colder and colder. Then dawn broke, steely, gray, with a flare in the east.

Jenet came back where she had left her master. Camp! She had grazed all night. Her sides that had been flat were now full. Jenet had weathered another vicissitude of her life. She stood for a while, in a daze, with one long ear down over her meek face. Jenet was waiting for Tappan, but he did not stir from under the long roll of canvas. Jenet waited. The winter sun rose in cold yellow flare. The snow glistened as with a crusting of diamonds. Somewhere in the distance sounded a long-drawn discordant bray. Jenet's ears shot up. She listened. She recognized the call of one of her kind. Instinct always prompted Jenet. Sometimes she did bray. Lifting her gray head, she sent forth a clarion: *Hee-haw hee-haw-haw . . . hee-haw how-e-e-e-e!*

That stentorian call started the echoes. They pealed down the slope and rolled out over the open country, clear as a bugle blast, yet hideous in their discordance. But this morning Tappan did not awaken.

★ ★ ★ ★ ★

Cañon Walls

★ ★ ★ ★ ★

I

"Wal, heah's another forkin' of the trail!" ejaculated Monty, as he sat cross-legged on his saddle and surveyed the prospect. "Thet Mormon shepherd back a ways gave me a good steer. But dog-gone it, I hate to impose on anyone, even Mormons."

The scene was Utah, north of the great cañon, with the wild ruggedness and magnificence of that region exemplified on all sides. Monty could see clear to the Pink Cliffs that walled the ranches and villages northward from this country of breaks. He had come up out of the abyss, across the desert between Mount Trumbull and Hurricane Ledge, and he did not look back. Kanab must be thirty or forty miles, as a crow flies, across this dotted valley of sage. But Monty did not know Utah, or anything of this north-rim country.

He rolled his last cigarette. He was hungry and worn out, and his horse was the same. Should he ride on to Kanab and throw in with one of the big cattle companies north of there or should he take to one of the lonely cañons and hunt for a homesteader in need of a rider? The choice seemed hard, because Monty was tired of gunfights, of two-bit rustling, of gambling, and other dubious means by which he had managed to live in Arizona. Not that Monty entertained any idea he had been really dishonest. He had the free-range cowboy's elasticity of judgment. He could find excuses even for his last escapade. But one or two more stunts like this last one at Longhill would make him an outlaw. He reflected that, if he were blamed for the Green Valley affair, also, which was not improbable, he might find himself an outlaw already, whether he agreed or not.

If he rode on to the ranches north, sooner or later someone from Arizona would come along; if he went down into the breaks of the cañon, he might find a job and a hiding place where he would be safe until the thing blew over and was forgotten. Then he would take good care not to fall into another. Bad company and a bottle had brought Monty to this pass, which he really believed was undeserved.

Monty dropped his leg back and slipped his boot into the stirrup. He took the trail to the left and felt relief. It meant that he was avoiding towns and ranches, outfits of curious cowboys, and others who might have undue interest in wandering riders.

In about an hour, as the shepherd had directed, the trail approached and ran along the rim of a cañon. Monty gazed down with approving eyes. The walls were steep and very deep, so deep that he could scarcely see the green squares of alfalfa, the orchards and pastures, the groves of cottonwoods, and a gray log cabin. He espied cattle and horses toward the upper end. At length the trail started down, and for a while then Monty lost his perspective, and, dismounting, he walked down the zigzag path, leading his horse.He saw, at length, that the cañon boxed here in a wild notch of cliff and thicket and jumbled wall, from under which a fine stream of water flowed. There were many acres that might have been under cultivation. Monty followed the trail along the babbling brook, crossed it above where the floor of the cañon widened and the alfalfa fields shone so richly green, and so on down a couple of miles to the cottonwoods. When he emerged from these, he was close to the cabin, and he could see where the cañon opened wide, with sheer red-gold walls, right out upon the desert. Indeed, it was a lonely retreat, far off the road, out of the grass country, a niche in colored cañon walls.

The cottonwoods were shedding their fuzzy seeds that like snow covered the ground. An irrigation ditch ran musically through the yard. Chickens, turkeys, calves had the run of the place. The dry odor of the cañon here appeared to take in the fragrance of wood smoke and baking bread.

Monty limped on, up to the cabin porch, which was spacious and comfortable, where no doubt the people who lived there spent many hours during fine weather. He espied a girl in the open door. She wore gray linsey, ragged and patched. His second glance made note of her superb build, her bare feet, her brown arms, and eyes that did not need half their piercing quality to see through Monty.

"Howdy, miss," hazarded Monty, although this was Mormon country.

"Howdy, stranger," she replied very pleasantly, so that Monty ceased looking for a dog.

"Could a thirsty rider get a drink around heah?"

"There's the brook. Best water in Utah."

"An' how about a bite to eat?"

"Tie up your horse and go 'round to the back porch."

Monty did as he was bidden, not without a couple more glances at this girl who, he observed, made no movement. But as he turned the corner of the house, he heard her call: "Ma, there's a tramp Gentile cowboy coming back for a bite to eat!"

When Monty reached the rear porch, another huge place under the cottonwoods, he was quite prepared to encounter the large woman, of commanding presence, but of more genial and kindly face.

"Good afternoon, ma'am," began Monty, lifting his sombrero. "Shore you're the mother to that girl out in front . . . you look alike an you're both arfel handsome . . . but I won't be took for no tramp Gentile cowpuncher."

The woman greeted him with a pleasant laugh. "So, young

man, you're a Mormon?"

"No, I ain't no Mormon, either. But particular, I ain't no tramp cowboy," replied Monty with spirit, and just then the young person who had roused it appeared in the back door with slow, curious smile. "I'm just lost an' tuckered out, an' hungry."

For reply she motioned to a pan and bucket of water on a nearby bench, and Monty was quick to take the hint, but performed his ablutions very slowly. When he came out of them, shivering and refreshed, the woman was setting a table for him and bade him take a seat.

"Ma'am, I only asked for a bite," he said.

"It's no matter. We've plenty."

Presently Monty sat down to a meal that surpassed any feast he ever attended. It was his first experience at a Mormon table, the fame of which was known on every range. He had to admit that distance and exaggeration had not lent enchantment here. Without shame he ate until he could hold no more, and, when he arose, he made the woman of the house a gallant bow.

"Lady, I never had such a good dinner in all my life," he said fervently. "An' I reckon it won't make no difference if I never get another. Just rememberin' this one will be enough."

"Blarney. You Gentiles shore have the gift of gab. Set down and rest a little."

Monty was glad to comply, and leisurely disposed his long, lithe, dusty self in a comfortable chair. He laid his sombrero on the floor, and hitched his gun around, and looked up, genially aware that he was being taken in by two pairs of eyes.

"I met a shepherd lad up on top an' he directed me to Andrew Boller's ranch. Is this heah the place?"

"No. Boller's is a few miles farther on. It's the first big ranch over the Arizona line."

"Shore I missed it. Wal, it was lucky for me. Are you near the Arizona line heah?"

"We're just over it."

"Oh, I see. Not in Utah a-tall," said Monty thoughtfully. "Any men about?"

"No. I'm the Widow Keitch, and this is my daughter Rebecca."

Monty guardedly acknowledged the introduction, without mentioning his name, an omission the shrewd, kindly woman noted. Monty was quick to feel that she must have had vast experience with men. The girl, however, wore an indifferent, rather scornful air.

"This heah is a good-size ranch . . . must be a hundred acres just in alfalfa," went on Monty. "You don't mean to tell me you two women run this ranch alone?"

"We do mostly. We hire the plowing, and we have to have firewood hauled. And we always have a boy around. But year in and out we do most of the work."

"Wal, I'll be darned!" ejaculated Monty. "Excuse me . . . but it shore is somethin' to heah. The ranch ain't so bad run-down at that. If you'll allow me to say so, Missus Keitch, it could be made a first-rate ranch. There's acres of uncleared land."

"My husband used to think so," replied the widow, sighing. "But since he's gone we have just managed to live."

"Wal, wal! Now I wonder what made me ride down the wrong trail . . . ? Missus Keitch, I reckon you could use a fine, young, sober, honest, hard-workin' cowboy who knows all there is about ranchin'."

Monty addressed the woman in cool, easy speech, quite deferential, and then he shifted his gaze to the dubious face of the daughter. He was discovering that it had a compelling charm. She laughed outright, as if to say what a liar he was. That not only discomfited Monty, but roused his ire. The Mormon baggage!

"I guess I could use such a young man," returned Mrs. Keitch shortly, with penetrating eyes on him.

"Wal, you're lookin' at him right now," said Monty fervently. "An' he's seein' nothin' less than the hand of Providence heah."

The woman stood up decisively. "Fetch your horse around," she said, and walked off the porch to wait for him. Monty made haste, his mind in a whirl. What was going to happen here? That girl! He ought to ride right on out of this cañon, and he was making up his mind to do that when he came back around the house to see that the girl had come to the porch rail. Her great eyes burned at his horse. Monty did not need to be told that she had a passion for horses. It would help some. But she did not appear to see Monty at all.

"You've a wonderful horse," said Mrs. Keitch. "Poor fellow. He's lame and tuckered out. We'll turn him loose in the pasture."

Monty followed her down a shady lane of cottonwoods, where the water ran noisily on each side, and he sort of trembled inwardly at the content of the woman's last words. He had heard of the Good Samaritan ways of Mormons. And in that short walk Monty did a deal of thinking. They reached an old barn beyond which lay a green pasture with an orchard running down one side. Peach trees were in bloom, lending a delicate and beautiful pink to the fresh spring foliage.

"What wages would you work for?" queried the woman earnestly.

"Wal, come to think of thet, for my board an' keep. Anyhow till we got the ranch payin'," replied Monty.

"Very well, stranger, that's a fair deal. Unsaddle your horse and stay," said the woman.

"Wait a minnit, lady," drawled Monty. "I got to substitute somethin' for that recommend I gave you. Shore I know cattle an' ranchin' backwards. But I reckon I should have said I'm a no-good, gun-throwin' cowpuncher who got run out of Arizona."

"What for?" demanded Mrs. Keitch.

"Wal, a lot of it was bad company an' bad licker. But at that I wasn't so drunk I didn't know I was rustlin' cattle."

"Why do you tell me?" she demanded.

"Wal, it is kinda funny. But I just couldn't fool a kind woman like you. Thet's all."

"You don't look like a hard-drinking man."

"Aw, I'm not. I never said so, ma'am. Fact is, I ain't much of a drinkin' cowboy a-tall."

"You came across the cañon?" she asked.

"Shore, an' by golly thet was the orfellest ride, an' slide, an' swim, an' climb I ever had. I really deserve heaven, lady."

"Any danger of a sheriff trailing you?"

"Wal, I've thought about that. I reckon one chance in a thousand."

"He'd be the first one I ever heard of . . . from across the cañon at any rate. This is a lonesome, out-of-the-way place . . . and, if you stayed away from the Mormon ranches and towns. . . ."

"See heah, lady," interrupted Monty sharply, "you shore ain't goin' to take me on?"

"I am. You might be a welcome change. Lord knows, I've hired every kind of a man. But not one of them ever lasted. You might."

"What was wrong with them?"

"I don't know. I never saw much wrong, but Rebecca could not get along with them, and she drove them away."

"Aw, I see!" exclaimed Monty, who did not see at all. "But I'm not one of the moonin' kind, lady, and I'll stick."

"All right. It's only fair, though, to tell you there's a risk. The young fellow doesn't live who could let Rebecca alone. It'd be a godsend to a distracted old woman."

Monty wagged his bare head, pondering, and slid the rim of

his sombrero through his fingers. "Wal, I reckon I've been most everythin' but a godsend, an' I'd shore like to try thet."

"What's your name?" she asked with those searching gray eyes on him.

"Monty Bellew . . . Smoke for short . . . an' it's shore shameful well known in some parts of Arizona."

"Any folks living?"

"Yes, back in Iowa. Father an' Mother gettin' along in years now. An' a kid sister growed up."

"You send them money every month, of course?"

Monty hung his head. "Wal, fact is, not so regular as I used to. Late years times have been hard for me."

"Hard, nothing! You've drifted into hard ways. Shiftless, drinking, gambling, shooting cowhand . . . now haven't you been just that?"

"I'm sorry, lady . . . I . . . I reckon I have."

"You ought to be ashamed. I know boys. I raised nine. It's time you were turning over a new leaf. Suppose we begin by burying that name Monty Bellew?"

"I'm shore willin' an' grateful, ma'am."

"Then it's settled. Tend to your horse. You can have the little cabin there under the big cottonwood. We've kept that for our hired help, but it hasn't been occupied much lately."

She left Monty then, and he stood a moment, irresolute. What a balance was struck there. Presently he slipped saddle and bridle off the horse, and turned him into the pasture. "Baldy, look at that alfalfa," he said. Weary as Baldy was, he lay down and rolled and rolled.

Monty carried his equipment to the tiny porch of the cabin under the huge cottonwood. He removed his saddlebags, which contained the meager sum of his possessions. Then he flopped down on the bench.

"Dog-gone it," he muttered. His senses seemed playing with

him. The leaves rustled above and the white cottonseeds floated down; the bees were murmuring; water tinkled swiftly by the porch; somewhere a bell on a sheep or calf broke the stillness. Monty had never felt such peace and tranquility, and his soul took on a burden of gratitude.

Suddenly a clear, resonant voice pealed out from the house. "Ma, what's the name of our new hand?"

"Ask him, Rebecca. I forgot to," replied the mother.

"If that isn't like you!"

Monty was on his way to the house and soon hove in sight to the young woman on the porch. He thrilled as he spied her, and he made himself some deep wild promises.

"Hey, cowboy. What's your name?" she called.

"Sam," he called back.

"Sam what?"

"Sam Hill."

"For the land's sake! That's not your name."

"Call me Land's Sake, if you like it better."

"*I* like it?" She nodded her curly head sagely, and she regarded Monty with a certainty that made him vow to upset her calculations or die in the attempt. She handed him a bucket. "Can you milk a cow?"

"I never saw my equal as a milker," asserted Monty.

"In that case I won't have to help," she replied. "But I'll go with you to drive in the cows."

II

From that hour dated Monty's apparent subjection. He accepted himself at Rebecca's valuation—that of a very small hired boy. Monty believed he had a way with girls, and at any rate that way had never been tried upon this imperious young Mormon miss. Monty made good his boast about being a master hand at the milking of cows. He surprised Rebecca, although she did not guess he saw it. For the rest Monty never looked at her—when she was looking—never addressed her, never gave her the slightest hint that her sex was manifest to him.

Now he knew perfectly well that his appearance did not tally with this kind of a cowboy. She realized it and was puzzled, but evidently he was a novelty. At first Monty sensed a slight antagonism of the Mormon against the Gentile, but in the case of Mrs. Keitch he never noticed this at all, and less and less from the girl.

The feeling of being in some sort of a trance persisted with Monty, and he could not account for it, unless it was the charm of this lonely Cañon Walls Ranch, combined with the singular attraction of its young mistress. Monty had not been there three days when he realized that sooner or later he would fall, and great would be the fall thereof. But his sincere and ever-growing admiration for Widow Keitch held him true to his inherent sincerity. It would not hurt him to have a terrible case over Rebecca, and he resigned himself. Nothing could come of it, except perhaps to chasten him. Ordinarily he would never let her dream of such a thing. She just gradually and imperceptibly grew on Monty. There was nothing strange in this. Wherever Monty had ridden, there had always been some girl before that he had bowed down. She might be a fright—a lanky, slab-sided, red-headed country girl, but that made no difference. His comrades had called him Smoke Bellew, because of his propensity for raising so much smoke where there was not any fire.

Sunday brought a change at the Keitch household. Rebecca appeared in a white dress, and Monty caught his breath. He worshipped from a safe distance through the leaves. Presently a two-seated buckboard drove up to the ranch house, and Rebecca lost no time climbing in with the young people. They drove off, of course, to church at the village of White Sage, some half dozen miles across the line. Monty thought it odd that Mrs. Keitch did not go.

There had been many a time in Monty's life when the loneliness and solitude of these dreaming cañon walls would have been maddening. But Monty found strange ease and solace here. He had entered upon a new era of thinking. He hated to think that it might not last. But it would last if the shadow of the past did not fall on Cañon Walls.

At 1:00 P.M. Rebecca returned with her friends in the buckboard, and presently Monty was summoned to dinner, by no less than Mrs. Keitch's trenchant call. Monty had not anticipated this, but he brushed and brightened himself up a bit, and proceeded to the house. Mrs. Keitch met him as he mounted the porch steps. "Folks," she announced, "this is our new man, Sam Hill. Sam, meet Lucy Card and her brother Joe, and Hal Stacey."

Monty bowed, and took the seat assigned to him by Mrs. Keitch. She was beaming, and the dinner table fairly groaned with the load of good things to eat. Monty defeated an overwhelming desire to look at Rebecca. In a moment he saw that the embarrassment under which he labored was silly. These Mormon young people were quiet, friendly, and far from curious. His presence at Widow Keitch's table was more natural to them than it seemed to Monty. Soon he was at ease and dared to glance across the table. Rebecca was radiant. How had it come that he had not seen her beauty? She appeared like a gorgeous, opening rose. Monty did not risk a second glance and he soliloquized to himself that he ought to go far up the cañon and crawl into a hole. Nevertheless, he enjoyed the dinner and did ample justice to it.

After dinner more company arrived, mostly on horseback. Sunday was evidently the Keitches' day at home. Monty made several unobtrusive attempts to escape, once being stopped in his tracks by a single glance from Rebecca, and the other times failing through the widow's watchfulness. He felt that he was very dense not to have seen sooner how they wished him to be at home. At length, toward evening, Monty left Rebecca to several of her admirers, who outstayed the other visitors, and went off for a sunset stroll under the cañon walls.

Monty did not consider himself exactly a dunce, but he could not see clearly through the afternoon's experience. There were, however, some points he could be sure of. The Widow Keitch had evidently seen better days. She did not cross the Arizona line into Utah. Rebecca was waited upon by a host of Mormons, to whom she appeared imperiously indifferent one moment and alluringly coy the next. She was a spoiled girl, Monty argued. Monty had not been able to discover the slightest curiosity or antagonism in those visitors, and, as they were all Mormons and he was a Gentile, it changed some preconceived ideas of his.

Next morning Monty plunged into the endless work needful to be done about the ranch. He doubled the water in the irrigation ditches, to Widow Keitch's delight. That day passed as if by magic. It did not end, however, without Rebecca's crossing Monty's trail, and earned for him a very good compliment from her, anent the fact that he might develop into a milkman.

The days flew by then, and another Sunday came, very like the first one, and that brought June around. Thereafter the weeks were as short as days. Monty was amazed to see what a diversity of tasks he could put an efficient hand to. But then he had seen quite a good deal of ranch service, aside from driving cattle. And it so happened that here was an ideal farm awaiting development, and Monty put his heart into the task. The summer was hot, especially in the afternoon under the reflected heat from the walls. He had cut alfalfa several times. And the harvest of fruit and grain was at hand. There were pumpkins so large that Monty could scarcely roll one over, bunches of grapes longer than his arm, great, luscious peaches that shone gold in the sunlight, and other farm products in proportion.

The womenfolk spent days putting up preserves, pickles, fruit. Monty used to go out of his way to smell the fragrant wood fire in the backyard under the cottonwoods, where the big, brass kettle steamed with peach butter. "I'll shore eat myself to death when winter comes," he said.

Among the young men who paid court to Rebecca were two brothers, Wade and Eben Tyler, lean-faced, still-eyed young Mormons who were wild-horse hunters. The whole southern end of Utah was run over by droves of wild horses, and according to some of the pioneers they would become a nuisance to the range. The Tylers took such a liking to Monty that they asked Mrs. Keitch to let him go with them on a hunt in October, over in what they called the Siwash. The widow was prevailed upon to consent, stipulating that Monty should fetch back a supply of venison. Rebecca said she would allow him to go if he brought her one of the wild mustangs with long mane and tail that touched the ground.

So when October rolled around, Monty rode off with the brothers, and three days brought them to the edge of a black forest called Buckskin. It took a whole day to ride through the magnificent spruces and pines to the rim of the cañon. Here, Monty found the wildest and most wonderful country he had ever seen. The Siwash was a rough section where the breaks in the rim afforded retreat for the thousands of deer and wild horses, and the cougars that preyed upon them. Monty had the hunt of his life, and, when those fleeting weeks were over, he and the Tylers were fast friends.

Monty returned to Cañon Walls Ranch, pleased to find that he had been sorely needed and missed, and keen to go at his work again. Gradually he thought less and less of that retreating

Arizona escapade that had made him a fugitive; a little time in that wild country had a tendency to make past things seem dim and far away. He ceased to start whenever he saw strange riders coming up the cañon gateway. Mormon sheepmen and cattlemen, when in the vicinity of Cañon Walls, always paid the Keitches a visit. Still Monty never ceased to pack a gun, a fact that Mrs. Keitch often mentioned. Monty said it was a habit.

He went to clearing the upper end of the cañon. The cottonwood, oak, and brush were as thick as a jungle. But it appeared to be mowed down under the sweep of Monty's axe. In his boyhood on the Iowa farm he had been a rail-splitter. How many useful things came back to him! Every day Rebecca or Mrs. Keitch or the boy Randy, who helped at chores, drove up in the big sled and hauled firewood. When the winter's wood, with plenty to spare, had been stored away, Mrs. Keitch pointed with satisfaction to a considerable saving of money.

The leaves did not fall until late in November, and then they changed color slowly and dropped reluctantly, as if not sure that winter could actually come to Cañon Walls. Monty doubted that it would. But frosty mornings did come, and soon thin skins of ice formed on the still pools. Sometimes, when Monty rode out of the cañon gateway upon the desert, he could see the white line reaching down from Buckskin, and Mount Trumbull had its crown of snow. But no real winter came to the cañon. The gleaming walls seemed to have absorbed enough of the summer sun to carry over. Every hour of daylight found Monty outdoors at one of the tasks that multiplied under his eye. After supper he would sit before the little stone fireplace he had built in his cabin, and watch the flames, and wonder about himself, and how long this could last. He did not see why it could not last always, and he went so far in calculation as to say that a debt paid cancelled even the acquiring of a few cattle not his own, in that past that got further back all the time. He had been just a wild cowboy, urged by drink and a need of money. He had asked only that it be forgotten and buried, but now he began to think he wanted to square that debt.

The winter passed, and Monty's labors had opened up as many new acres as had been cleared originally. Cañon Walls Ranch took the eye of Andrew Boller who made Widow Keitch a substantial offer for it. Mrs. Keitch laughed her refusal, and the remark she made to Boller mystified Monty for many a day. Something like Cañon Walls someday being as great a ranch as that one of which the Church had deprived her!

Monty asked Wade Tyler what she'd meant, and Wade replied that he had heard how John Keitch had owed the bishop money, and the great ranch, after Keitch's death, had been taken. But that was one of the few questions Monty ever asked. The complexity and mystery of the Mormon Church did not interest him. It had been a shock, however, to find that two of Mrs. Keitch's Sunday callers, openly courting Rebecca's hand, already had wives. *By golly, I ought to marry her myself*, declared Monty with heat, as he soliloquized to himself beside his fire, and then he laughed at his dreaming conceit. He was only the hired help to Rebecca.

How good to see the green burst out upon the cottonwoods, and then the pink on the peach trees! Monty had been at Cañon Walls a year. It seemed incredible. He could see a vast change in the ranch. And what transformation had that labor wrought in him!

"Sam, we're going to need help this spring," said Mrs. Keitch. "We'll want a couple of men and a teamster . . . a new wagon."

"Wal, we shore need aplenty," drawled Monty, "an' I reckon we'd better think hard."

"This ranch is overflowing with milk and honey. Sam, you've made it bloom. We must make a deal. I've spoken to you before, but you always put me off. We ought to be partners."

"There ain't any hurry, lady," replied Monty. "I'm happy heah, an' powerful set on makin' the ranch go big. Funny no farmer hereabouts ever saw its possibilities. Wal, thet's our good luck."

"Boller wants my whole alfalfa cut this year," went on Mrs. Keitch. "Saunders, a big cattleman . . . no Mormon, by the way . . . is ranging south. And Boller wants to gobble all the feed. How much alfalfa can we cut this year?"

"Countin' the new acreage upward of two hundred tons."

"Sam Hill!" she cried incredulously.

"Wal, you needn't Sam Hill me. I get enough of that from Rebecca. But you can gamble on the ranch from now on. We have the soil an' the sunshine . . . twice as much an' twice as hot as these farmers out in the open. An' we have water. Lady, we're goin' to grow things."

"It's a dispensation of the Lord!" she exclaimed fervently.

"Wal, I don't know aboot that, but I can guarantee results. We start new angles this spring. There's a side cañon up heah that I cleared. Just the place for hogs. You know what a waste of fruit there was last fall. We'll not waste anythin' from now on. We can raise food enough to pack this cañon solid with turkeys, chickens, hogs."

"Sam, you're a wizard, and the Lord merely guided me that day I took you in," replied Mrs. Keitch. "We're independent now and I see prosperity ahead. When Andrew Boller offered to buy this ranch, I saw the handwriting on the wall."

"You bet. An' the ranch is worth twice what he offered."

"Sam, I've been an outcast, in a way, but this will sweeten my cup."

"Wal, lady, you never made me no confidences, but I always took you for the happiest woman I ever seen," declared Monty stoutly.

At this juncture the thoughtful Rebecca Keitch, who had listened as was her habit, spoke feelingly: "Ma, I want a lot of new dresses. I haven't a decent rag to my back. And look there!" She stuck out a shapely foot, bursting from an old shoe. "I want to go to Salt Lake City and buy things. And if we're not so poor any more. . . ."

"My dearest, *I* cannot go to Salt Lake," interrupted the mother in amaze and sorrow.

"But I can. Sue Tyler is going with her mother," burst out Rebecca, passionately glowing.

"Of course, Daughter, you must have clothes to wear. And I have long thought of that. But to go to Salt Lake? I don't know. It worries me. Sam, what do you think of Rebecca's idea?"

"Which one?" asked Monty.

"About going to Salt Lake to buy clothes."

"Perfectly ridiculous," replied Monty blandly.

"Why?" flashed Rebecca, turning upon him with great eyes aflame.

"Wal, you don't need no clothes in the first place. . . ."

"Don't I?" demanded Rebecca hotly. "You bet I don't need any clothes for *you*. You never look at me. I could go around here positively stark naked and you'd never even see me."

"An' in the second place," went on Monty with a wholly assumed imperturbability, "you're too young an' too crazy aboot boys to go on such a long journey alone."

"Daughter, I . . . I think Sam is right," rejoined the mother.

"I'm eighteen years old!" screamed Rebecca. "And I wouldn't be going alone."

"Sam means you should have a man with you."

Rebecca stood a moment in speechless rage, then she broke down. "Why doesn't the damn' fool . . . offer to take me . . . then?"

"Rebecca!" cried Mrs. Keitch in horror.

Monty, meanwhile, had been undergoing a remarkable transformation. "Lady, if I was her dad. . . ."

"But you're not," sobbed Rebecca.

"There, Daughter . . . and maybe next year you *could* go to Salt Lake," added Mrs. Keitch consolingly.

Rebecca made a miserable compromise, an acceptance rendered vastly significant to Monty by the deep, dark look she gave him as she flounced away.

"Oh, dear," sighed Mrs. Keitch. "Rebecca is a good girl. Now she often flares up like that and lately she has been queer. If she'd only set her heart on some man."

III

Monty had his doubts about the venture to which he had committed himself. But he undertook it willingly enough, because Mrs. Keitch was tremendously pleased and relieved. She evidently feared this high-spirited girl. As it happened, Rebecca rode to Kanab with the Tylers, with the understanding that she would return on Monty's wagon.

The drive took Monty all day and there was a good deal of upgrade. He did not believe he could make the thirty miles back in daylight hours, unless he got a very early start, and he just about knew he never could get Rebecca Keitch to leave Kanab before dawn. Still the whole prospect was one of adventure, and much of Monty's old devil-may-care spirit seemed to rouse to meet it.

He camped on the edge of town, and next morning drove in and left the old wagon at a blacksmith shop for repairs. The four horses were turned into pasture. Then Monty went about executing Mrs. Keitch's instructions, which had to do with engaging helpers, and numerous purchases. That evening saw a big, new, shiny wagon at the blacksmith shop, packed full of flour, grain, hardware, supplies, harness, and what-not. The genial storekeeper who waited upon Monty averred that this Keitch must have had her inheritance returned to her. All the Mormons were kindly interested in Monty and his work at Cañon Walls, which had become talk all over the range. They were likable men, except the gray-whiskered old patriarchs who belonged to another day. Monty did not miss seeing several very pretty Mormon girls, and their notice of him pleased Monty immensely when Rebecca happened to be around to see.

Monty ran into her every time he entered a store. She spent all the money she had saved up, and all her mother had given her, and she borrowed the last few dollars he had.

"Shore, you're welcome," said Monty in reply to her thanks. "But ain't you losin' your haid a little?"

"Well, so long's I don't lose it over *you*, what do you care?" she retorted gaily with a return of that dark glance that had mystified him.

Monty replied that her mother had expressly forbidden her to go into debt for anything.

"Don't you try to boss me, Sam Hill," she warned, but she was still too happy to be angry.

"Rebecca, I don't care two bits what you do," said Monty shortly.

"Oh, don't you? Thanks. You always flattered me," she returned mockingly. It struck Monty then that she knew something about him or about herself that he did not share.

"We'll be leavin' before sunup," he added briefly. "You'd better let me have all your bundles so I can take them out to the wagon an' pack them tonight."

Rebecca demurred, but would not give a reason, which must have meant that she wanted to gloat over her purchases. Monty finally prevailed upon her, and it took two trips for him, and a boy he had hired, to carry the stuff out to the blacksmith's.

"Lord, if it should rain!" ejaculated Monty, happening to

think that he had no extra tarpaulin. So he went back to the store and got one, and hid it, with the purpose of having fun with Rebecca in case a storm threatened.

After supper Rebecca drove out to Monty's camp with some friends.

"I don't like this. You should have gone to the rim," she said loftily.

"Wal, I'm used to campin'," he drawled.

"Sam, they're giving a dance for me tonight," announced Rebecca.

"Fine. Then you needn't go to bed a-tall, an' we can get an early start."

The young people with Rebecca shouted with laughter, and she looked dubious.

"Can't we stay over another day?"

"I should smile we cain't," retorted Monty with unusual force. "An' if we don't get an early start, we'll never reach home tomorrow. So you just come along heah, young lady, aboot four o'clock."

"In the morning?"

"In the mawnin'. I'll have some breakfast for you."

It was noticeable that Rebecca made no rash promises. Monty rather wanted to give in to her—she was so happy and gay—but he remembered his obligations to Mrs. Keitch, and remained firm.

As they drove off, Monty's sharp ears caught Rebecca complaining: ". . . and I can't do a solitary darn' thing with that Arizona cowpuncher."

This rather pleased Monty, as it gave him distinction, and was proof that he had not yet betrayed himself to Rebecca. He would proceed on these lines.

That night he did a remarkable thing, for him. He found out where the dance was being held, and peeped through a window to see Rebecca in her glory. He did not miss, however, the fact that she did not outshine several other young women there. Monty stifled a yearning that had not bothered him for a long time. *Dog-gone it! I ain't no old gaffer. I could dance the socks off some of them Mormons.* He became aware presently that between dances the young Mormon men came outside and indulged in fist fights. He could not see any reason for these encounters, and it amused him. *Gosh, I wonder if thet's just a habit with these hombres. Fact is, though, there's shore not enough girls to go 'round. Holy Mackerel, how I'd like to have my old dancin' pards heah! Wouldn't we wade through thet corral? I wonder what's become of Slim an' Cuppy, an' if they ever think of me. Dog-gone.*

Monty sighed and returned to camp. He was up before daylight, but not in any rush. He had a premonition what to expect. Day broke and the sun tipped the low desert in the east, while Monty leisurely got breakfast. He kept an eye on the look-out for Rebecca. The new boy, Jake, arrived with shiny face, and later one of the men engaged by Mrs. Keitch came. Monty had the two teams fetched in from pasture, and hitched up. It was just as well that he had to wait for Rebecca, because the new harness did not fit and required skilled adjustment, but he was not going to tell her that. The longer she made him wait, the longer would be the scolding she would get.

About 9:00 A.M. she arrived in a very much overloaded buckboard, gay of attire and face, and so happy that Monty, had he been sincere, could never have reproved her. But he did it, very sharply, and made her look like a chidden child before her friends. This reacted upon Monty so pleasurably that he began afresh. But this was a mistake.

"Yah! Yah! Yah! Yah!" she screamed at him. And her friends let out a roar of merriment.

"Becky, you shore have a tip-top chaperon," remarked one frank-faced Mormon boy. And other remarks were not wanting to hint that one young rider in the world had not succumbed to Rebecca.

"Where am I going to ride?" she asked curtly.

Monty indicated the high driver's seat: "Unless you'd rather ride with them two new hands on the other wagon."

Rebecca scorned to give reasons, but climbed to the lofty perch.

"Girls, it's nearer heaven than I've ever been yet!" she called gaily.

"What do you mean, Becky?" replied a pretty girl with roguish eyes. "So high up . . . or because . . . ?"

"Go along with you," interrupted Rebecca with a blush. "You think of nothing but men. I wish you had . . . but good bye . . . good bye. I've had a lovely time."

Monty clambered to the driver's seat, and followed the other wagon out of town, down into the desert. Rebecca appeared moved to talk.

"Oh, it was a change. I had a grand time. But I'm glad you wouldn't let me go to Salt Lake. It'd have ruined me, Sam."

Monty felt subtly flattered, but he chose to remain aloof, and disapproving.

"Nope. Hardly thet. You was ruined long ago, Miss Rebecca," he drawled.

"Don't call me 'miss,' " she flashed. "And see here, Sam Hill . . . do you hate us Mormons?"

"I shore don't. I like all the Mormons I've met. They're just fine. An' your ma is the best woman I ever knew."

"Then I'm the only Mormon you've no use for," she retorted with bitterness. "Don't deny it. I'd rather you didn't add falsehood to your . . . your other faults. It's a pity, though, that we can't get along. Mother depends on you now. You've certainly pulled us out of a hole. And I . . . I'd like you . . . if you'd let me. But you always make me out a wicked, spoiled girl. Which

I'm not. Why couldn't you come to the dance last night? They wanted you. Those girls were eager to meet you."

"I wasn't asked . . . not that I'd've come anyhow," stammered Monty.

"You know perfectly well that in a Mormon town or house you are welcome," she said. "What did you want? Would you have had me stick my finger in the top hole of your vest and look up at you like a dying duck and say . . . 'Sam, please come?' "

"My Gawd, no. I never dreamed of wantin' you to do anythin'," replied Monty hurriedly. He was getting over his depth here, and began to doubt his ability to say the right things.

"Why not? Am I hideous? Aren't I a human being? A *girl?*" she queried with resentful fire.

Monty deliberated a moment, as much to recover his scattered wits as to make adequate reply. "Wal, you shore are a live human creature. An' as handsome as any girl I ever seen. But you're spoiled somethin' turrible. You're the most awful flirt I ever watched, an' the way you treat these fine Mormon boys is shore scandalous. You don't know what you want more'n one minnit straight runnin'. An' when you get what you want, you're sick of it right then."

"Oh, is that *all?*" she burst out, and then followed with a peal of riotous laughter. But she did not look at him or speak to him again for hours.

Monty liked that better. He had the thrill of her presence, without her disturbing chatter. The nucleus of a thought tried to wedge into his consciousness—that this girl was not indifferent to him. But he squelched it.

At noon they halted in a rocky depression, where water filled the holes, and Rebecca got down to sit in the shade of a cedar.

"I want something to eat," she declared imperiously.

"Sorry, but there ain't nothin'," replied Monty imperturbably as he mounted to the seat again. The other wagon rolled on, cracking the rocks under its wheels.

"Are you going to starve me into submission?"

Monty laughed at her. "Wal, I reckon if someone took a willow switch to your bare legs an' . . . wal, he might get a little submission out of you."

"You're worse than a Mormon!" she cried in disgust as if that was the end of iniquity.

"Come on, child," said Monty with pretended weariness. "If we don't keep steppin' along lively, we'll never get home to-night."

"Good! I'll delay you as much as I can. Sam, I'm scared to death to face Mother." And she giggled.

"What about?"

"I went terribly in debt. But I didn't lose my 'haid' as you say. I thought it all out. I won't be going again for ages. And I'll work. Then the change in our fortunes tempted me."

"Wal, I reckon we can get around tellin' your mother," said Monty lamely.

"You wouldn't give me away, Sam?" she asked in surprise with strange, intent eyes. She got up to come to the wagon.

"No, I wouldn't. 'Course not. What's more, I can lend you the money . . . presently."

"Thanks, Sam. But I'll tell Mother."

She got up and rode beside him for miles without speaking. It seemed nothing to Monty, to ride in that country and keep silent. The desert was not conducive to conversation. It was so sublime as to be oppressive. League after league of rock and sage, of black ridge and red swale, and always the great landmarks looming as if unattainable. Behind them the Pink Cliffs rose higher the farther they got, to their left the long, black fringe of the Buckskin gradually climbed into obscurity, to the fore rolled away the colored desert, an ever-widening bowl that led the gaze to the purple chaos in the distance—that wild region of the rent earth called the cañon country.

Monty did not tell Rebecca that they could not get even halfway home, and that they would have to camp. But mentally, as a snow squall formed on the Buckskin, he told her it likely would catch up with them and turn to rain.

"Oh, Sam!" she wailed, aghast. "If my things got wet!"

He did not give her any assurance or comfort, and about midafternoon, when the road climbed toward a divide, he saw that they would not miss the storm. But he would go in camp at the pines and could weather it.

Before sunset they reached the highest point along the road, from which the spectacle down toward the west made Monty acknowledge that he was gazing at the grandest panorama ever presented to his enraptured eyes. He was a Nature-loving cowboy of long years on the open range.

Rebecca watched with him, and he could feel her absorption. Finally she sighed and said, as if to herself: "One reason I'll marry a Mormon . . . if I have to . . . is that I never want to leave Utah."

They halted in the pines, low down on the far side of the divide, where a brook brawled merrily, and here the storm, half rain and half snow, caught them. Rebecca was frantic. She did not even know where her treasures were packed.

"Oh, Sam, I'll never forgive you!"

"*Me?* What have I got to do with it?" he queried in pretended amazement.

"Oh, you *knew* it would rain," she said. "And if you'd been half a man . . . if you didn't *hate* me, you . . . you could have saved my things."

"Wal, if thet's how you feel aboot it, I'll see what I can do," he drawled.

In a twinkling he jerked out the tarpaulin and spread it over the new wagon where he had carefully packed her cherished belongings, and in the same twinkling her woebegone face changed to astonished beatitude. Monty thought she might kiss him and he was scared stiff.

"Ma was right, Sam. You are the wonderfullest fellow," she said. "But . . . why didn't you *tell* me?"

"I forgot, I reckon. Now this rain ain't goin' to amount to much. After dark it'll turn off cold. I put some hay in the bottom of the wagon heah, an' a blanket. So you can sleep comfortable."

"*Sleep!* Sam, you're not going to stop here?"

"Shore am. This new wagon is stiff, an' the other one heavy loaded. We're darned lucky to reach this good campin' spot."

"But, Sam, we can't stay here. We must drive on. It doesn't make any difference how *long* we are, so that we keep moving."

"An' kill our horses, an' then not get in? Sorry, Rebecca. If you hadn't delayed us five hours, we might have done it, allowin' for faster travel in the cool of mawnin'."

"Sam, do you want to ruin me?" she asked with great, childish, accusing eyes on him.

"Wal! Rebecca Keitch, if you don't beat me! I'll tell you what, miss. Where I come from, a man can entertain honest desire to spank a crazy girl without havin' evil intentions."

"You can spank me to your heart's content . . . but . . . Sam . . . take me home."

"Nope. I can fix it with your ma, an' I cain't see thet it amounts to a darn otherwise."

"Any Mormon girl who laid out on the desert . . . all night with a Gentile . . . would be ruined!" she declared.

"But we're not alone!" yelled Monty, red in the face. "We've got a man an' boy with us."

"No Mormon would ever . . . believe it," sobbed Rebecca.

"Wal, then, to hell with the Mormons who won't!" exclaimed

Monty, exasperated beyond endurance.

"Mother will make you marry me," ended Rebecca with such tragedy of eye and voice that Monty could not but believe such a fate would be horrible.

"Aw, don't distress yourself, Miss Keitch," responded Monty with profound dignity. "I couldn't be druv to marry you . . . not to save your precious Mormon Church . . . nor the whole damn' world of Gentiles from . . . from conflagration!"

IV

Next day Monty drove through White Sage at noon, and reached Cañon Walls about midafternoon, completing a journey he would not want to undertake again under like circumstances. He made haste to unburden himself to his beaming employer.

"Wal, Missus Keitch, I done aboot everythin' as you wanted," he said. "But I couldn't get an early start yestiddy mawnin', an' so we had to camp at the pines."

"Why couldn't you?" she demanded, as if seriously concerned.

"Wal, for several reasons, particular thet the new harness wouldn't fit."

"You shouldn't have kept Rebecca out all night," said the widow severely.

"I don't see how it could have been avoided," replied Monty mildly. "You wouldn't have had me kill four horses?"

"Did you stop at White Sage?"

"Only to water, an' we didn't see no one."

"Maybe we can keep the Mormons from finding out," returned Mrs. Keitch with relief. "I'll talk to those new hands. Mormons are close-mouthed when it's to their interest."

"Wal, lady, heah's the receipts, an' my notes on expenditures," added Monty, handing them over. "My pore haid shore rang over all them figgers. But I got the prices you wanted. I found out you gotta stick to a Mormon. But he won't let you buy from another storekeeper, if he can help it."

"Indeed, he won't. Well, Daughter, what have you to say for yourself? I expected to see you with the happiest of faces. But you look like you used to, when you stole jam. I hope it wasn't your fault Sam had to keep you all night on the desert."

"Yes, Ma, it was," admitted Rebecca, and, although she spoke frankly, she plainly feared her mother.

"So. And Sam wouldn't tell on you, eh?"

"No, it seems he wouldn't . . . *wonderful* to see. Come in, Ma, and let me confess the rest . . . while I've the courage."

The mother looked grave. Monty saw that her anger would be a terrible thing.

"Lady, don't be hard on the girl," he said with his easy drawl and smile. "Just think. She hadn't been to Kanab for two years. Two years! An' she a growin' girl. Kanab is some shucks of a town. I was surprised. An' she was just a kid let loose."

"Sam Hill! So you have fallen into the ranks, at last!" ejaculated Mrs. Keitch, while Rebecca telegraphed him a passionately grateful glance.

"Lady, I don't just savvy that aboot the ranks," replied Monty stiffly. "But I've fallen from grace all my life. Thet's why I'm . . ."

"No matter," interrupted the widow hostilely, and it struck Monty that she did not care to have him confess such facts before Rebecca. "Unpack the wagons and put the things on the porch, except what should go to the barn."

Monty helped the two new employees to unpack the old wagon first, and then directed them to the barn. Then he removed Rebecca's many purchases and piled them on the porch, all the while his ears burned at the heated argument going on within. Rebecca grew less and less vociferous while the mother gained, until she harangued her daughter terribly. It ended presently with the girl's uncontrolled sobbing. Monty drove out to the barn, disturbed in mind.

"Dog-gone! She's hell when she's riled," he soliloquized. "Now I wonder which it was. Rebecca spendin' all her money an' mine, an' then runnin' up bills . . . or because she made us stay a night out . . . or mebbe it's somethin' I don't know aboot. *Whew,* but she laid it on thet pore kid. Dog-gone the old Mormon! She'd better not pitch into me."

Supper was late that night and the table was set in the dusk. Mrs. Keitch had regained her composure, but Rebecca had a woebegone face, pallid from weeping. Monty's embarrassment seemed augmented by the fact that she squeezed his hand. But it was a silent meal, soon finished, and, while Rebecca reset the table for the new employees, Mrs. Keitch drew Monty aside on the porch. It suited him just as well that dusk was deepening into night.

"I am pleased with the way you carried out my instructions," said Mrs. Keitch. "I could not have done so well. My husband John was never any good in business. You are shrewd, clever, and reliable. If this year's harvest shows anything near what you claim, I can do no less than make you my partner. There is nothing to prevent us from developing another cañon ranch. John had a lien on one west of here. It's bigger than this and uncleared. We could acquire that, if you thought it wise. In fact, we could go far. Not that I am money-mad, like many Mormons, but I would like to show them. What do you think about it, Sam?"

"Wal, I agree, 'cept makin' me full pardner seems more'n I deserve. But if the crops turn out big this fall . . . an' you can gamble on it . . . I'll make a deal with you for five years or ten or life."

"Thank you. That is well. It insures comfort in my old age as

121

well as something substantial for my daughter. Sam, do you understand Rebecca?"

"Good Lord, no!" exploded Monty.

"I reckoned you didn't. Do you realize that where she is concerned you are wholly unreliable?"

"What you mean, lady?" he queried, thunderstruck.

"She can wind you 'round her little finger."

"Huh! She just cain't do anythin' of the sort," declared Monty, trying to get angry. She might ask a question presently that would be exceedingly hard to answer.

"Perhaps you do not know it. That'd be natural. At first I thought you a deep, clever cowboy, one of the devil-with-the-girls kind, and that you would give Rebecca the lesson she deserves. But now I think you a soft-hearted, easy-going, *good* young man, actually stupid about a girl."

"Aw, thanks, lady," replied Monty, most uncomfortable, and then his natural spirit rebelled. "I never was accounted all that stupid aboot Gentile girls."

"Rebecca is no different from any girl. I should think you'd have seen that the Mormon style of courtship makes her sick. It is too simple, too courteous, too respectful, and too importantly religious to stir her heart. No Mormon will ever get Rebecca, unless I force her to marry him. Which I have been pressed to do and which I should never want to do."

"Wal, I respect you for thet, lady," replied Monty feelingly. "But why all this talk about Rebecca? I'm shore sympathetic, but how does it concern me?"

"Sam, I have not a friend in all this land, unless it's you."

"Wal, you can shore gamble on me. If you want I . . . I'll marry you an' be a dad to this girl who worries you so."

"Bless your heart! No, I'm too old for that, and I would not see you sacrifice yourself. But, oh, wouldn't that be fun . . . and revenge?"

"Wal, it'd be heaps of fun." Monty laughed. "But I don't reckon where the revenge would come in."

"Sam, you're given me an idea," spoke up the widow in a thrilling whisper. "I'll threaten Rebecca with this. That I could marry you and make you her father. If that doesn't chasten her . . . then the Lord have mercy upon me."

"She'd laugh at you."

"Yes. But she'll be scared to death. I'll never forget her face one day when she confessed you said she should be switched . . . well, it was quite shocking, if you said it."

"I shore did, lady," he admitted.

"Well, we begin all over again from today," concluded the widow thoughtfully. "To build anew. Go back to your work and plans. I have utmost confidence in you. My troubles are easing. But I have not one more word of advice about Rebecca."

"I can't say as you gave me any advice a-tall. But mebbe thet's because I'm stupid. Thanks, Missus Keitch, an' good night."

The painful, pondering hour Monty put in that night, walking in the moonlit shadow under the gleaming walls, only augmented his quandary. He ended it by admitting he was in love with Rebecca, ten thousand times worse than he had ever loved any girl before, and that she could wind him around her little finger. If she knew! But he swore he would never, never let her find it out.

Next day seemed the inauguration of a new regime at Cañon Walls. The ranch had received an impetus, like that given by water run over rich, dry ground. Monty's hours were doubly full. Always there was Rebecca, singing on the porch at dusk— "In the gloaming, oh, my darling"—a song that rushed Monty back to home in Iowa, and the zigzag rail fences, or she was at this elbow during the milking hour, an ever-growing task, or in the fields. She could work, that girl, and he told her mother it would not take long for her to earn the money she had squandered.

Sunday after Sunday passed, with the host of merry callers, and no word was ever spoken of Rebecca having passed a night on the desert with a Gentile. So that specter died, except in an occasional mocking look she gave him that, he interpreted, meant she could still betray herself and him.

In June came the first cutting of alfalfa—fifty acres with an enormous yield. The rich, green, fragrant hay stood knee-high. Monty tried to contain himself. But it did seem marvelous that the few simple changes he had made could produce such a harvest.

Monty worked late, and a second bell did not deter him. He wanted to finish this last great stack of alfalfa. Then he espied Rebecca, running along the trail, calling. Monty let her call. It somehow tickled him, pretending not to hear. So she came out in the field and up to him.

"Sam, are you deaf? Mother rang twice. And then she sent me."

"Wal, I reckon I been feelin' awful good aboot this alfalfa," he replied.

"Oh, it is lovely. So dark and green. So sweet to smell! Sam, I'll just have to slide down that haystack."

"Don't you dare!" called Monty in alarm.

But she ran around to the lower side and presently appeared on top, flushed, full of fun and desire to torment him.

"Please, Rebecca, don't slide down. You'll topple it over, an' I'll have all the work to do again."

"Sam, I'll just have to, like I used to when I was a kid."

"You're a kid right now," he retorted. "Go back an' get down careful."

She shrieked and let herself go and came sliding down, rather at the expense of modesty. Monty knew he was angry, but he feared he was some other things.

"There! You see how slick I did it? I could always beat the girls . . . and boys, too."

"Wal, let thet do," growled Monty.

"Just one more, Sam."

He dropped his pitchfork and made a lunge for her, catching only the air. How quick she was. He controlled an impulse to run after her. Soon she appeared on top again, with something added to her glee.

"Rebecca, if you slide down heah again, you'll be sorry," he said warningly.

"What'll *you* do?"

"I'll spank you."

"Sam Hill! You wouldn't dare."

"So help me heaven, I will."

She did not in the least believe him, but it was evident that his threat made her project only the more thrilling. There was at least a possibility of events.

"Look out. I'm coming!" she cried with a wild, sweet trill of laughter.

As she slid down, Monty leaped to intercept her. A scream escaped Rebecca, but it was because of her treacherous skirts. That did not deter Monty. He caught her and held her high off the ground, and there he pinioned her.

Whatever Monty's intent had been, it escaped him. A winged flame flicked at every fiber of his being. He had her arms spread, and it took all his strength and weight to hold her there, feet off the ground. She was not in the least frightened at this close contact, although a wonderful speculation sparkled in her big gray eyes.

"You caught me. Now what?" she said challengingly.

Monty kissed her squarely on the mouth.

"Oh!" she cried, divinely startled. Then a rush of scarlet

waved up from the rich, gold swell of her neck. She struggled. "Let me down . . . you Gentile cowpuncher!"

Monty kissed her again, longer, harder than before. Then, when she tried to scream, he stopped her lips again.

"You . . . little Mormon . . . devil!" he panted. "This heah . . . was shore . . . comin' to you."

"I'll kill you!"

"Wal, it'll be worth . . . dyin' for." Then Monty kissed her until she gasped for breath, and, when she sagged, limp and unresisting, in his arms, he kissed her cheeks, her eyes, her hair, and like a madness whose hunger had been augmented by what it fed on he went back to her red, parted lips.

Suddenly all appeared to grow dark. A weight carried him down with the girl. The top of the alfalfa stack had slid down upon them. Monty floundered out and dragged Rebecca from under the fragrant mass. She did not move. Her eyes were closed. With trembling hand he brushed the leaves and seeds of alfalfa off her white face. But her hair was full of them.

"My Gawd, I've played hob now," he whispered, as the enormity of his offence dawned upon him. Nevertheless he felt a tremendous drag at him as he looked down on her. Only her lips had a vestige of color. Suddenly her eyes opened wide. From the marvel of them Monty fled.

V

Monty's first wild impulse, as he ran, was to get out of the cañon, away from the incomprehensible forces that had worked such havoc with him. His second was to rush to Mrs. Keitch and confess to her, before Rebecca could damn him forever in the good woman's estimation. Then by the time he reached his cabin and fell on the porch, those impulses had given place to others. But it was not Monty's nature to be long helpless. Presently he sat up, wringing wet with sweat, and still shaking.

"Aw, what come over me?" he breathed hoarsely. And suddenly he realized that nothing so terrible had happened. He had been furious when he held her, close and tight, with those challenging eyes and lips right at his. All else except the sweetness of momentary possession had gone into eclipse. He loved the girl and had not had any realization of the magnitude of his love. He believed he could explain to Mrs. Keitch, so that she would not drive him away. But, of course, he would be dirt under Rebecca's feet from that hour on. Yet, even in his mournful acceptance of this fate, his spirit rose resentfully to wonder and inquire about this Mormon girl.

Darkness had almost set in. Down the land Monty saw a figure approaching, quite some distance, and he thought he heard a low voice singing. But Rebecca would be weeping.

"Re-becca!" called Mrs. Keitch from the porch, in her mellow, far-reaching voice.

"Coming, Ma," replied the girl.

Monty sank into the shadow of his little cabin. He felt small enough to be unseen, but dared not risk it. And he watched in fear and trepidation. Suddenly Rebecca's low contralto voice rang on the quiet, sultry air.

> In the gloaming,
> Oh, my darling
> When the lights are
> dim and low
> And the flickering shadows falling
> Softly come and softly go.

Monty's heart swelled to bursting. Did she realize the truth and was she mocking him? He was simply flabbergasted. But how the sweet voice filled the cañon and came back in echo from the walls.

127

Rebecca, entering the square between the orchards and the cottonwoods, gave Monty's cabin a wide berth.

"Isn't Sam with you?" called Mrs. Keitch from the porch.

"Sam? No, he isn't."

"Where is he? Didn't you call him? Supper's getting cold."

"I haven't any idea where Sam is. Last I saw of him, he was running like mad," rejoined Rebecca with a giggle.

That giggle saved Monty a stroke of apoplexy.

"Running? What for?" queried the mother as Rebecca mounted the porch.

"Mother, it was the funniest thing. I called Sam, but he didn't hear. I went out to tell him supper was ready. He had a great, high stack of alfalfa up. Of course, I wanted to climb it and slide down. Well, Sam got mad and ordered me not to do any such thing. Then I *had* to do it. Such fun! Sam growled like a bear. Well, I couldn't resist climbing up for another slide. Do you know, Mother, Sam got perfectly furious. He has a terrible temper. He commanded me not to slide off that stack. And when I asked him what he'd do if I did . . . he declared he'd spank me. Imagine! I only meant to tease him. I wasn't going to slide at all. Then you could see I *had* to. So I did. I . . . oh, dear! . . . I fetched the whole top of the stack down on us . . . and, when I got out from under the smothering hay . . . and could see . . . there was Sam, running for dear life."

"Well, for the land's sake!" ejaculated Mrs. Keitch dubiously, and then she laughed. "You drive the poor fellow wild with your pranks. Rebecca, will you never grow up?" Whereupon she came out to the porch rail and called: "Sam!"

Monty started up, opened his door to let it slam, and replied, in what he thought the funniest voice: "Hello?"

"Hurry to supper."

Monty washed his face and hands, brushed his hair, while his mind whirled. Then he sat down bewildered. *Dog-gone me! Can you beat that girl? She didn't give me away. She didn't lie, yet she never told. . . . She's not goin' to tell. Must have been funny to her. But shore it's a daid safe bet she never got kissed thet way before. I just cain't figger her out.*

Presently he went to supper and was grateful for the dim light. Still he felt the girl's eyes on him. No doubt she was now appreciating him as a real Arizona Gentile rowdy cowboy. He pretended weariness, and soon hurried away to his cabin, where he spent a night of inexplicable dreams and waking emotions. Remorse, however, had died a natural death after Rebecca's story to her mother.

With dawn came the blessed work into which Monty plunged, finding all relief except oblivion. Rebecca did not speak a single word to him for two weeks. Mrs. Keitch finally remarked it and reproved her daughter.

"Speak to *him?*" asked Rebecca in haughty amaze. "Maybe . . . when he crawls on his knees!"

"But, Daughter, he only threatened to spank you. And I'm sure you gave him provocation. You must always forgive. We cannot live at enmity here," said the good mother persuasively.

Then she turned to Monty.

"Sam, you know Rebecca has passed eighteen and she feels an exaggerated sense of maturity. Perhaps if you'd tell her you were sorry. . . ."

"What aboot?" asked Monty, when she hesitated.

"Why, about what offended Rebecca."

"Aw, shore. I'm awful sorry," drawled Monty, his keen eyes on the girl. "Turrible sorry . . . but it's aboot not sayin' an' doin' *more* . . . an' then spankin' her to boot."

Mrs. Keitch looked aghast, and, when Rebecca ran away hysterical with mirth, she seemed positively nonplussed.

"That girl! Why, Sam, I thought she was furious with you. But she's not. It's sham."

"Wal, I reckon she's riled all right, but it doesn't matter. An'
see heah, lady," he went on, lowering his voice, "I'm confidin' in
you an' if you give me away . . . wal, I'll leave the ranch. I reckon
you've forgot how you told me I'd lose my haid over Rebecca.
Wal, I've lost it, clean an' plumb an' otherwise. An' sometimes I
do queer things. Just remember thet's why. This won't make no
difference. I'm happy heah. Only I want you to understand
me."

"Sam Hill," she whispered in ecstatic amaze. "So that's what
ails you? Now all will be well."

"Wal, I'm glad you think so," replied Monty shortly. "An' I
reckon it will be . . . when I get over these growin' pains."

She leaned toward him. "My son, I understand now. Rebecca
has been in love with you for a long time. Just let her alone. All
will be well."

Monty gave her one mute, incredulous stare, and then he
fled. In the darkness of his cabin he persuaded himself of the
absurdity of the sentimental Mrs. Keitch's claim. Then he could
sleep. But when day came again, he found the harm had been
wrought. He lived in a kind of dream and he was always watching for Rebecca.

Straightway he began to make discoveries. Gradually she
came out of her icy shell. She worked as usual, and apparently
with less discontent, especially in the mornings when she had
time to sew on the porch. She would fetch lunch to the men
out in the fields. Often Monty saw her on top of a haystack, but
he always quickly looked away. She climbed the wall trail; she
gathered armloads of wildflowers. She helped where her help
was not needed.

On Sundays, she went to church at White Sage and in the
afternoon entertained callers. But it was noticeable that her
Mormon courtiers grew fewer as the summer advanced. Monty
missed in her the gay allure the open coquetry, the challenge

that had once been marked.

All this was thought-provoking for Monty, but nothing to the discovery that Rebecca watched him from afar and when near at hand. Monty could not credit it. Only another instance of his addled brain. It happened, moreover, that the eyes that had made Monty Smoke Bellew a great shot and tracker, wonderful out on the range, could not be deceived. The hour he lent himself, in stifling curiosity, to spying upon Rebecca he learned the staggering truth.

In the mornings and evenings, while he was at work near the barn or resting on his porch, she watched him, thinking herself unseen. She peeped from behind her window curtain, through the leaves, above her sewing, from the open doors—from everywhere the great, gray, hungry eyes sought him. It began to get on Monty's nerves. Did she hate him so that she planned some dire revenge? But the eyes that watched him in secret seldom or never met his own any more. Sometimes his consciousness took hold of Mrs. Keitch's strangely tranquil words, and then he had to battle fiercely to recover his equilibrium. The last asinine thing Smoke Bellew could ever do would be to give in to vain obsession. But the situation invoked and haunted him.

One noonday Monty returned to his cabin to find a magical change in his single room. He could not recognize it. Clean and tidy and colorful it flashed at him. There were Indian rugs on the clay floor, Indian ornaments on the log walls, curtains at his windows, a scarf on his table, and a gorgeous bedspread on his bed. In a little Indian vase on the table stood some stalks of golden daisies and purple asters.

"What happened around heah this mawnin'?" he drawled at meal hour. "My cabin is spruced up so fine."

"Yes, it does look nice," replied Mrs. Keitch complacently. "Rebecca has had that in mind for some time."

"Wal, it was turrible good of her," said Monty.

"Oh, nonsense," returned Rebecca with a swift blush. "Ma wanted you to be more comfortable."

"Ma did? How you trifle with the precious truth, Daughter! Sam, I never thought of it, I'm ashamed to say."

Monty escaped somehow, as he always managed to escape when catastrophe impended. But one August night when the harvest moon rose, white and grand, above the black cañon rim, he felt such a strange, impelling presentiment he could not leave his porch and go in to bed. It had been a hard day—one in which the accumulated cut of alfalfa had mounted to unbelievable figures. Cañon Walls Ranch, with its soil and water and Sam, was simply a gold mine. All over southern Utah the ranchers were clambering for that alfalfa.

The hour was late. The light in Rebecca's room had long been out. Frogs and owls and night hawks had ceased their lonely calls. Only the insects hummed in the melancholy stillness.

A rustle startled Monty. Was it a leaf falling from a cottonwood? A dark form crossed the barred patches of moonlight. Rebecca! She passed close to him as he lounged on the porch steps. Her face flashed white. She ran down the lane and stopped to look back.

"Dog-gone! Am I drunk or crazy or just moonstruck?" ejaculated Monty, rising. "What is that girl up to? Shore she seen me heah. Shore she did."

He started down the lane, and, when he came out of the shadow of the cottonwoods into the moonlight, she ran fleetly as a deer. But again she halted and looked back. Monty stalked after her. He was roused now. He would see this thing through. If it were another of her hoydenish tricks. . . . But there seemed to be an appalling something in this night flight out into the cañon under the full moon.

Monty lost sight of her at the end of the lane. But when he reached it and turned into the field, he espied her far out, lingering, looking back. He could see her moon-blanched face. She ran on, and he followed.

That side of the cañon lay clear in the silver light. On the other the looming cañon wall stood up black, with its last rim moon-fired against the sky. The alfalfa shone brightly, yet kept its deep dark, rich, velvety hue.

Rebecca was making for the upper end where that day the alfalfa had been cut. She let Monty gain on her, but at last with a wild trill she ran to the huge, silver-shining haystack and began to climb it.

Monty did not run; he slowed down. He did not know what was happening to him, but his state seemed to verge upon lunacy. One of his nightmares! He would awaken presently. But then the white form edged up the steep haystack. He had finished this mound of alfalfa with the satisfaction of an artist.

When he reached it, Rebecca had not only gained the top, but was lying flat, propped on her elbows. Monty went closer—right up to the stack. He could see her distinctly now, scarcely fifteen feet above his head. The moonlight lent her an exceeding witchery. But it was the mystery of her eyes that seemed to end all for Monty. Why had he followed her? He could do nothing. His threat was but an idle memory. His anger would not rise. She would make him betray his secret and then, alas, Cañon Walls could no longer be a home for him.

"Howdy, Sam," she said in a tone that he could not comprehend,

"Rebecca, what does this mean?" he asked.

"Isn't it a glorious night?"

"Yes. But the hour is late. An' you could have watched from your window."

"Oh, no. I had to be out in it. Besides, I wanted to make you follow me."

"Wal, you shore have. I was plumb scared, I reckon. An' . . . an' I'm glad it was only fun. But why did you want me to follow you?"

"For one thing I wanted you to see me climb your new haystack."

"Yes? Wal, I've seen you. So come down now. If your mother should ketch us out heah. . . ."

"And I wanted you to see me slide down *this* one."

The silvery medium that surrounded this dark-eyed witch was surely charged with intense and troubled potentialities for Monty. He was lost and he could only look the query she expected.

"And I wanted to see terribly . . . what you'd do," she went on, with a seriousness that must have been mockery.

"Rebecca, child, I will do . . . nothin'," replied Monty almost mournfully.

She got to her knees, and leaned as if to see him closer. Then she turned around to sit down and slid to the very edge. Her hands were clutched, deep in the alfalfa.

"You won't spank me, Sam?" she asked in impish glee.

"No. Much as I'd like to . . . an' as you shore need it . . . I cain't."

"Bluffer. Gentile cowpuncher . . . showing yellow . . . marble-hearted fiend!"

"Not thet last, Rebecca. For all my many faults, not thet," he said sadly.

She seemed fighting to let go of something that the mound of alfalfa represented only in symbol. Surely the physical effort for Rebecca to hold her balance there could not account for the strain of body and face. All the mystery of Cañon Walls and the beauty of the night hovered over her.

"Sam, dare me to slide," she taunted.

"No," he retorted grimly.

"Coward."

"Shore. You hit me on the haid there."

Then ensued a short silence. He could see the quivering. She was moving, almost imperceptibly. Her eyes, magnified by the shadow and light, transfixed Monty.

"Gentile, dare me to slide . . . into your arms!" she cried a little huskily.

"Mormon witch! Would you . . . ?"

"Dare me!"

"Wal, I dare . . . you, Rebecca . . . but, so help me Gawd, I won't answer for consequences."

Her laugh, like that other sweet, wild trill, pealed up, but now full of joy, of certainty, of surrender. And she let go her hold, to spread wide her arms, and come sliding on an avalanche of silver hay down upon him.

VI

Next morning, Monty found work in the fields impossible. He roamed about like a man possessed, and at last went back to the cabin. It was just before the noonday meal. Rebecca hummed a tune while she set the table. Mrs. Keitch sat on her rocker, busy with work on her lap. There was no charged atmosphere. All seemed serene.

Monty responded to the girl's sly glance by taking her hand and leading her up to her mother.

"Lady," he began hoarsely, "you've knowed long my feelin's for Rebecca. But it seems . . . she . . . she loves me, too. How thet come aboot I cain't say. It's shore the wonderfulest thing. Now, I ask you, for Rebecca's sake most . . . what can be done about this heah trouble?"

"Daughter, is it true?" asked Mrs. Keitch, looking up with

serene and smiling face.

"Yes, Mother," replied Rebecca simply.

"You love Sam?"

"Oh, I do."

"Since when?"

"Always, I guess. But I never knew till this June."

"I am very glad, Rebecca," replied the mother, rising to embrace her. "As you could not or would not love one of your own creed, it is well that you love this man who came a stranger to our gates. He is strong, he is true, and what his religion is matters little."

Then she smiled upon Monty. "My son, no man can say what guided your steps to Cañon Walls. But I have always felt God's intent in it. You and Rebecca shall marry."

"Oh, Mother," murmured the girl rapturously, and she hid her face.

"Wal . . . I'm willin' . . . an' happy," stammered Monty. "But I ain't worthy of her, lady, an' you know that old. . . ."

She silenced him. "You must go to White Sage and be married at once."

"At once! When?" faltered Rebecca.

"Aw, Missus Keitch, I . . . I wouldn't hurry the girl. Let her have her own time."

"No, why wait? She has been a strange, starved creature. Tomorrow you must take her, Sam."

"Wal an' good, if Rebecca says so," said Monty with wistful eagerness.

"Yes," she whispered. "Will you go with me, Mother?"

"Yes," suddenly rang out Mrs. Keitch as if inspired. "I will go. I will cross the Utah line once more before I am carried over. But not White Sage. We will go to Kanab. You shall be married by the bishop."

In the excitement and agitation that possessed the mother

and daughter then Monty sensed a significance more than just the tremendous importance of an impending marriage. Some deep, strong motive urged Mrs. Keitch to go to Kanab, there to have her bishop marry Rebecca to a Gentile. One way or another it did not matter to Monty. He rode in the clouds. He could not believe in his good luck. Never in his life had he touched real happiness until then.

The womenfolk were an hour late in serving lunch, and during that the air of vast excitement permeated their every word and action.

"Wal, this heah seems like a Sunday," said Monty, after the hasty meal. "I've loafed a lot this mawnin'. But I reckon I'll go back to work now."

"Oh, Sam, don't . . . when . . . when we're leaving so soon," remonstrated Rebecca shyly.

"When are we leavin'?"

"Tomorrow . . . early."

"Wal, I'll get that alfalfa up anyhow. It might rain, you know. Rebecca, do you reckon you could get up at daylight for this heah ride?"

"I could stay up all night, Sam."

Mrs. Keitch laughed at them. "There's no rush. We'll start after breakfast. And get to Kanab early enough to make arrangements for the wedding next day. It will give Sam time to buy a respectable suit of clothes to be married in."

"Dog-gone. I hadn't thought of thet," replied Monty ruefully.

"Sam Hill, you won't marry *me* in a ten-gallon hat, a red shirt, blue overalls, and boots," declared Rebecca.

"How about wearin' my gun?" drawled Monty.

"Your gun!" exclaimed Rebecca.

"Shore. You've forgot how I used to pack it. I might need it over there among them Mormons who're crazy about you."

"Heavens! You leave that gun home."

Monty went his way, marveling at the change in his habits and in his life. Next morning, when he brought the buckboard around, Mrs. Keitch and Rebecca appeared radiant of face, gorgeous of apparel. But for the difference in age anyone might have mistaken the mother for the intended bride.

The drive to the Kanab with fresh horses and light load took six hours. The news spread over Kanab like wildfire in dry prairie grass. For all Monty's keen eyes, he never caught a jealous look, nor did he hear a nasty word. That settled with him the status of the Keitches. Mormon friends. The Tyler brothers came into town and made much of the fact that Monty would soon be one of them, and they planned another fall hunt for wild mustangs and deer. Waking hours sped by and sleeping hours were few. Almost before Monty knew what was happening he was in the presence of the august bishop.

"Will you come into the Mormon Church?" asked the bishop.

"Wal, sir, I cain't be a Mormon," replied Monty in perplexity. "But I shore have respect for you people an' your church. I reckon I never had no religion. I can say I'll never stand in Rebecca's way, in anythin' pertainin' to hers."

"In the event she bears you children, you will not seek to raise them Gentiles?"

"I'd leave that to Rebecca," replied Monty sagely.

"And the name Sam Hill, by which you are known, is a middle name?"

"Shore, just a cowboy middle name."

So they were married. Monty feared they would never escape from the many friends and the curious crowd. But at last they were safely in the buckboard, speeding homeward. Monty sat in the front seat alone. Mrs. Keitch and Rebecca occupied the rear seat. The girl's expression of pure happiness touched Monty and made him swear deeply in his throat that he would try to deserve her. Mrs. Keitch had evidently lived through one of the few great events of her life. What dominated her feelings, Monty could not divine, but she had the look of a woman who asked no more. Somewhere a monstrous injustice or wrong had been done the Widow Keitch. Recalling the bishop's strange look at Rebecca—a look of hunger—Monty pondered deeply. The ride home, being downhill with a pleasant breeze off the desert and that wondrous panorama coloring and smoking as the sun set, seemed all too short for Monty. He drawled to Rebecca, when they reached the portal of Cañon Walls and halted under the gold-leaved cottonwoods: "Wal, wife, heah we are home. But we shore ought to have made thet honeymoon drive a longer one."

That supper time was the only one in which Monty ever saw Widow Keitch bow her head for the salvation of these young people so strongly brought together, for the home overflowing with milk and honey, for the hopeful future.

They had their fifth cutting of alfalfa in September, and it was in the nature of an event. The Tyler boys rode over to help, fetching Sue to visit Rebecca. And there was merrymaking. Rebecca would climb over mounds of alfalfa and slide down, screaming her delight. And once she said to Monty: "Young man, you should pray under every haystack you build."

"Ahuh. An' what for should I pray, Rebecca?" he drawled.

"To give thanks for all this sweet-smelling alfalfa has brought you."

The harvest gods smiled on Cañon Walls that autumn. Three wagons plied between Kanab and the ranch for weeks, hauling the produce that could not be used. While Monty went off with the Tyler boys for their hunt on the Buckskin, the womenfolk and their guests, and the hired hands, applied themselves industriously to the happiest work of the year—preserving all they could of the luscious yield of the season.

Monty came back to a home such as had never been his even

in dreams. Rebecca was incalculably changed, and so happy that Monty trembled as he listened to her sing, as he watched her work. The mystery never ended for him, not even when she whispered that they might expect a little visit from the angels next spring. But Monty's last doubt faded, and he gave himself over to work, to his loving young wife, to waltz in the dusk under the gleaming walls, to a lonely pipe beside his little fireside.

The winter passed, and spring came, doubling former activities. They had taken over the cañon three miles to the westward, which, once cleared of brush and cactus and rock, promised well. The problem had been water and Monty solved it. Good fortune had attended his every venture.

Around the middle of May, when the cottonwoods were green and the peach trees pink, Monty began to grow restless about the coming event. It uplifted him one moment, appalled him the next. In that past that seemed so remote now he had snuffed out life. Young, fiery, grim Smoke Bellew! And by some incomprehensible working out of life he was about to become a father.

On the 17th of June, some hours after breakfast, he was hurriedly summoned from the fields. His heart appeared to choke him.

Mrs. Keitch met him at the porch. He scarcely knew her.

"My son, do you remember this date?"

"No," replied Monty wonderingly.

"Two years ago today you came to us. And Rebecca has just borne you a son."

"Aw . . . my Gawd! Have . . . how is she, lady?" he gasped.

"Both well. We could work no more. It has all been a visitation of God. Come."

Some days later the important matter of christening the youngster came up.

"Ma wants one of those jaw-breaking Biblical names," said Rebecca, pouting. "But I like just plain Sam."

"Wal, it ain't much of a handle for such a wonderful boy."

"It's your name. I love it."

"Rebecca, you kinda forget Sam Hill was just a . . . a sort of a middle name. It ain't my real name."

"Oh, yes, I remember now," replied Rebecca, her great eyes lighting. "At Kanab . . . the bishop asked about Sam Hill. Mother had told him this was your nickname."

"Darlin', I had another nickname once," he said sadly.

"So, my man of mysterious past, and what was that?"

"They called me Smoke."

"How funny! Well, I may be Missus Monty Smoke Bellew, according to the law and the church, but *you*, my husband, will still always be Sam Hill."

"An' the boy?" asked Monty, enraptured.

"Is Sam Hill, too."

An anxious week passed, and then all seemed surely well with the new mother and the baby. Monty ceased to tiptoe around. He no longer awoke with a start in the dead of night.

Then one Saturday as he came out on the wide front porch, at a hello from someone, he saw four riders. A bolt shot back from a closed door of his memory. Arizona riders! How well he knew the lean faces, the lithe shapes, the gun belts, the mettlesome horses!

"Nix, fellers!" called the foremost rider as Monty came slowly out.

An instinct and a muscular contraction passed over Monty. Then he realized he packed no gun and was glad. Old habit might have been too strong. His hawk eye saw lean hands drop from hips. A sickening, terrible despair followed his first reaction.

"Howdy, Smoke," drawled the foremost rider.

"Wal, dog-gone! If it ain't Jim Sneed," returned Monty as he recognized the sheriff, and he descended the steps to walk out and offer his hand, quick to see the swift, penetrating gray eyes run over him.

"Shore, it's Jim. I reckoned you'd know me. Hoped you would, as I wasn't keen about raisin' your smoke."

"Ahuh. What you-all doin' over heah, Jim?" asked Monty, with a glance at the three watchful riders.

"Main thing I come over for was to buy stock for Strickland. An' he said, if it wasn't out of my way, I might fetch you back. Word come that you've been seen in Kanab. An' when I made inquiry at White Sage, I shore knowed who Sam Hill was."

"I see. Kinda tough it happened to be Strickland. Dog-gone! My luck just couldn't last."

"Smoke, you look uncommon fine," said the sheriff, with another appraising glance. "You shore haven't been drinkin'. An' I seen first off you wasn't totin' no gun."

"That's all past for me, Jim."

"Wal, I'll be damned!" ejaculated Sneed, and fumbled for a cigarette. "Bellew, I just don't savvy."

"Reckon you wouldn't, Jim. I'd like to ask if my name ever got linked up with that Green Valley deal two years an' more ago?"

"No, it didn't, Smoke, I'm glad to say. Your pards, Slim an' Cuffy, pulled that. Slim was killed coverin' Cuffy's escape."

"Ahuh. So Slim . . . wal, wal . . . ," sighed Monty, and paused a moment to gaze into space.

"Smoke, tell me your deal here," said Sneed.

"Shore. But would you mind comin' indoors?"

"Reckon I wouldn't. But, Smoke, I'm still figgerin' you the cowboy."

"Wal, you're way off. Get down an' come in."

Monty led the sheriff into Rebecca's bedroom. She was

awake, playing with the baby, and both looked lovely. "Jim, this is my wife an' youngster," said Monty feelingly. "An' Rebecca, this heah is an old friend of mine, Jim Sneed, from Arizona."

That must have been a hard moment for the sheriff—the cordial welcome of the blushing wife, the smiling mite of a baby who hung onto his finger, the atmosphere there of unadulterated joy. At any rate, when they went out again to the porch, Sneed wiped his perspiring face and swore at Monty: "God damn it. Cowboy, have you gone an' double-crossed that sweet girl?"

Monty told him the few salient facts of his romance, and told it with trembling eagerness to be believed.

"So you've turned Mormon?" ejaculated the sheriff.

"No, but I'll be true to these women. An' one thing I ask, Sneed. Don't let it be known in White Sage or anywhere over heah *why* I'm with you. I can send word to my wife I've got to go. Then afterward I'll come back."

"Smoke, I wish I had a stiff drink," replied Sneed. "But I reckon you haven't any thin'."

"Only water an' milk."

"Good Lawd! For an Arizonian!" Sneed halted at the head of the porch steps and shot out a big hand. His cold eyes had warmed. "Smoke, may I tell Strickland you'll send him some money now an' then . . . till thet debt is paid?"

Monty stared and faltered. "Jim . . . you shore can."

"Fine," returned the sheriff in a loud voice, and he strode down the steps to mount his horse. "*Adiós,* cowboy. Be good to thet little woman."

Monty could not speak. He watched the riders down the lane, out into the road, and through the looming cañon gates to the desert beyond. His heart was full. He thought of Slim and Cuffy, those young firebrand comrades of his range days. He could remember now without terror. He could live once more with his phantoms of the past. He could see lean, lithe Arizona riders come into Cañon Walls, if that happy event ever chanced, and he was glad.

★ ★ ★ ★ ★

From Missouri

★ ★ ★ ★ ★

I

With jingling spurs a tall cowboy stalked out of the post office to confront his three comrades crossing the wide street from the saloon opposite.

"Look heah," he said, shoving a letter under their noses. "Which one of you longhorns has wrote her again?"

From a gay careless trio his listeners suddenly grew blank, then intensely curious. They stared at the handwriting on the letter.

"Tex, I'm a son-of-a-gun if it ain't from Missouri!" ejaculated Andy Smith, his lean red face bursting into a smile.

"It shore is," declared Nevada.

"From Missouri!" echoed Panhandle Ames.

"Wal?" queried Tex, almost with a snort.

The three cowboys jerked up to look from Tex to one another, and then back at Tex.

"It's from *her*," went on Tex, his voice hushing on the pronoun. "You-all know thet handwritin'. Now how aboot this deal? We swore none of us would write ag'in to this heah school-marm. Some one of you has double-crossed the outfit."

Loud and unified protestations of innocence emanated from his comrades. But it was evident Tex did not trust them, and that they did not trust him or each other.

"Say, boys," said Panhandle suddenly. "I see Beady in there lookin' darn' sharp at us. Let's get off in the woods somehow."

"Back to the bar," replied Nevada. "I reckon us'll all need

stimulants."

"Beady!" ejaculated Tex, as they turned across the street. "He could be to blame as much as any of us."

"Shore. It'd be more like Beady," replied Nevada. "But, Tex, your mind ain't workin'. Our lady friend from Missouri has wrote before without gettin' any letter from us."

"How do we know thet?" demanded Tex suspiciously. "Shore the boss's typewriter is a puzzle, but it could hide tracks. Savvy, pards?"

"Gee, Tex, you need a drink," returned Panhandle peevishly.

They entered the saloon and strode to the bar, where from all appearances Tex was not the only one to seek artificial stimulus strength. Then they repaired to a corner, where they took seats and stared at the letter Tex threw down before them.

"From Missouri, all right," said Panhandle wearily, studying the postmark. "Kansas City, Missouri."

"It's her writin'," added Nevada in awe. "Shore I'd know thet out of a million letters."

"Ain't you goin' to read it to us?" queried Andy Smith.

"Mister Frank Owens," replied Tex, reading from the address on the letter. "Springer's Ranch. Beacon, Arizona. . . . Boys, this heah Frank Owens is all of us."

"Huh! Mebbe he's a darn' sight more," added Andy.

"Looks like a low-down trick we're to blame for," resumed Tex, seriously shaking his hawk-like head. "Heah he reads in a Kansas City paper aboot a schoolteacher wantin' a job out in dry Arizonie. And he ups an' writes her an' gets her a-rarin' to come. Then, when she writes an' tells us she's *not over forty,* then us quits like yellow coyotes. An' we four anyhow shook hands on never writin' her again. Wal, somebody did, an' I reckon you-all think me as big a liar as I think you. But thet ain't the point. Heah's another letter to Mister Owens an' I'll bet my saddle it means trouble. Shore, I'm plumb afraid to read it."

"Say, give it to me," demanded Andy. "I ain't afraid of any woman."

Tex snatched the letter out of Andy's hand.

"Cowboy, you're too poor educated to read letters from ladies," observed Tex. "Gimme a knife, somebody. . . . Say, it's all perfumed."

Tex impressively spread out the letter and read laboriously:

Kansas City, Mo.
June 15
Dear Mr. Owens:

Your last letter has explained away much that was vague and perplexing in your other letters.

It has inspired me with hope and anticipation. I shall not take time now to express my thanks, but hasten to get ready to go West. I shall leave tomorrow and arrive at Beacon on June 19 at 4:30 P.M. You see I have studied the timetable.

Yours very truly,
Jane Stacey

Profound silence followed Tex's perusal of the letter. The cowboys were struck dumb. But suddenly Nevada exploded.

"My Gawd, fellers, today's the Nineteenth!"

"Wal, Springer needs a schoolmarm at the ranch," finally spoke up the practical Andy. "There's half a dozen kids growin' up without any schoolin', not to talk about other ranches. I heard the boss say this hisself."

"Who the hell did it?" demanded Tex in a rage with himself and his accomplices.

"What's the sense in hollerin' aboot thet now?" returned Nevada. "It's done. She's comin'. She'll be on the Limited.

Reckon us're got five hours. It ain't enough. What'll we *do?*"

"I can get awful drunk in thet time," contributed Panhandle nonchalantly.

"Ahuh. An' leave it all to us," retorted Tex scornfully. "But we got to stand pat on this heah deal. Don't you know this is Saturday an' thet Springer will be in town?"

"Aw, Lord! We're all goin' to get fired," declared Panhandle. "Serves us right for listenin' to you, Tex. Us can all gamble this trick hatched in your head."

"Not my haid more'n yours or anybody," returned Tex hotly.

"Say, you locoed cowpunchers," interposed Nevada. "What'll we do?"

"Shore is bad," sighed Andy. "What'll we do?"

"We'll have to tell Springer."

"But, Tex, the boss'd never believe us about not followin' the letters up. He'd fire the whole outfit."

"But he'll have to be told somethin'," returned Panhandle stoutly.

"Shore he will," went on Tex. "I've an idea. It's too late now to turn this poor schoolmarm back. An' somebody'll have to meet her. Somebody's got to borrow a buckboard an' drive her out to the ranch."

"Excuse me!" replied Andy. And Panhandle and Nevada echoed him. "I'll ride over on my hoss, an' see you-all meet the lady," Andy added.

Tex had lost his scowl, but he did not look as if he favorably regarded Andy's idea. "Hang it all!" he burst out hotly. "Can't some of you gents look at it from her side of the fence? Nice fix for any woman, I say. Somebody ought to get it good for this mess. If I ever find out. . . ."

"Go on with your grand idea," interposed Nevada.

"You-all come with me. I'll get a buckboard. I'll meet the lady an' do the talkin'. I'll let her down easy. An' if I cain't head her back, we'll fetch her out to the ranch an' then leave it up to Springer. Only we won't tell her or him or anybody who's the real Frank Owens."

"Tex, that ain't so plumb bad," declared Andy admiringly.

"What *I* want to know is who's goin' go do the talkin' to the boss?" queried Panhandle. "It mightn't be so hard to explain now. But after drivin' up to the ranch with a woman! You-all know Springer's shy. Young an' rich, like he is, an' a bachelor . . . he's been fussed over so he's plumb afraid of girls. An' here you're fetchin' a middle-aged schoolmarm who's romantic an' mushy! My Gawd, I say send her home on the next train."

"Pan, you're wise on hosses an' cattle, but you don't know human nature, an' you're daid wrong about the boss," rejoined Tex. "We're in a bad fix, I'll admit. But I lean more to fetchin' the lady up than sendin' her back. Somebody down Beacon way would get wise. Mebbe the schoolmarm might talk. She'd shore have cause. An' suppose Springer hears about it . . . that some of us or all of us played a low-down trick on a woman. He'd be madder at that than if we fetched her up. Likely he'll try to make amends. The boss may be shy on girls but he's the squarest man in Arizona. My idea is we'll deny any of us is Frank Owens, an' we'll meet Miss . . . Miss . . . what was that there name? . . . Miss Jane Stacey and fetch her up to the ranch, an' let her do the talkin' to Springer."

During the next several hours, while Tex searched the town for a buckboard and team he could borrow, the other cowboys wandered from the saloon to the post office and back again, and then to the store, the restaurant, and all around. The town had gradually filled up with Saturday visitors.

"Boys, there's the boss," suddenly broke out Andy, pointing, and he ducked into the nearest doorway, which happened to be that of another saloon. It was half full of cowboys, ranchers, Mexicans, tobacco smoke, and noise.

Andy's companions had rushed pell-mell after him, and not until they all got inside did they realize that this saloon was a rendezvous for cowboys decidedly not on friendly terms with Springer's outfit. Nevada was the only one of the trio who took the situation nonchalantly.

"Wal, we're in, an' what the hell do we care for Beady Jones an' his outfit," he remarked, quite loud enough to be heard by others besides his friends.

Naturally they lined up at the bar, and this was not a good thing for young men who had an important engagement and who must preserve sobriety. After several rounds of drinks had appeared, they began to whisper and snicker over the possibility of Tex meeting the boss.

"If only it doesn't come off until Tex gets our forty-year-old schoolmarm from Missouri with him in the buckboard!" exclaimed Panhandle in huge glee.

"Shore. Tex, the handsome galoot, is most too blame for this mess," added Nevada. "Thet cowboy won't be above makin' love to Jane, if he thinks we're not around. But, fellows, we want to be there."

"Wouldn't miss seein' the boss meet Tex for a million," said Andy.

Presently a tall striking-looking cowboy, with dark face and small bright eyes like black beads, detached himself from a group of noisy companions, and confronted the trio, more particularly Nevada.

"Howdy, men," he greeted them, "what you-all doin' in here?"

He was coolly impertinent, and his action and query noticeably stilled the room. Andy and Panhandle leaned back against the bar. They had been in such situations before and knew who would do the talking for them.

"Howdy, Jones," replied Nevada coolly and carefully. "We happened to bust in here by accident. Reckon we're usually more particular what kind of company we mix with."

"Ahuh! Springer's outfit is shore a stuck-up one," sneered Beady Jones in a quite loud tone. "So stuck up they won't even ride around drift fences."

Nevada slightly changed his position.

"Beady, I've had a couple of drinks an' ain't very clear-headed," drawled Nevada. "Would you mind talkin' so I can understand you?"

"*Bah!* You savvy all right," declared Jones sarcastically. "I'm tellin' you straight what I've been layin' to tell your yaller-headed Texas pard."

"Now you're speakin' English, Beady. Tex an' me are pards, shore. An' I'll take it kind of you to get this talk out of your system. You seem to be chock-full."

"You bet I'm full an' I'm a-goin' to bust!" shouted Jones, whose temper evidently could not abide the slow cool speech with which he had been answered.

"Wal, before you bust, explain what you mean by Springer's outfit not ridin' around drift fences."

"Easy. You just cut through wire fences," retorted Jones.

"Beady, I hate to call you a low-down liar, but that's what you are."

"You're another!" yelled Jones. "I seen your Texas Jack cut our drift fence."

Nevada struck out with remarkable swiftness and force. He knocked Jones over upon a card table, with which he crashed to the floor. Jones was so stunned that he did not recover before some of his comrades rushed to him, and helped him up. Then, black in the face and cursing savagely, he jerked for his gun. He got it out, but, before he could level it, two of his friends seized him, and wrestled with him, talking in earnest alarm. But Jones fought them.

"Ya damn' fool!" finally yelled one of them. "He's not packin' a gun. It'd be murder."

That brought Jones to his senses, although certainly not to calmness.

"Mister Nevada . . . next time you hit town you'd better come heeled," he hissed between his teeth.

"Shore. An' thet'll be bad for you, Beady," replied Nevada curtly.

Panhandle and Andy drew Nevada out to the street, where they burst into mingled excitement and anger. Their swift strides gravitated toward the saloon across from the post office.

When they emerged sometime later, they were arm in arm, and far from steady on their feet. They paraded up the one main street of Beacon, not in the least conspicuous on a Saturday afternoon. As they were neither hilarious nor dangerous, nobody paid any attention to them. Springer, their boss, met them, gazed at them casually, and passed without sign of recognition. If he had studied the boys closely, he might have received an impression that they were hugging a secret, as well as each other.

In due time the trio presented themselves at the railroad station. Tex was there, nervously striding up and down the platform, now and then looking at his watch. The afternoon train was nearly due. At the hitching rail below the platform stood a new buckboard and a rather spirited team of horses.

The boys, coming across the wide square, encountered this evidence of Tex's extremity, and struck a posture before it.

"Livery stable outfit, by gosh," said Andy.

"Son-of-a-gun if it ain't," added Panhandle with a huge grin.

"Thish here Tex spendin' hish money royal," agreed Nevada.

Then Tex espied them. He stared. Suddenly he jumped straight up. After striding to the edge of the platform, with face as red as a beet, he began to curse them.

"Whash mashes, ole pard?" asked Andy, who appeared a little

less stable than his comrades.

Tex's reply was another volley of expressive profanity. And he ended with: ". . . you-all yellow quitters to get drunk an' leave me in the lurch. But you gotta get away from heah. I shore won't have you aboot when thet train comes."

"Tex, your boss ish in town lookin' for you," said Nevada.

"I don't care a damn," replied Tex with fire in his eye.

"Wait till he shees you," gurgled Andy.

"Tex, he jest ambled past us like we wasn't gennelmen," added Panhandle. "Never sheen us a-tall."

"No wonder, you drunken cowpunchers," declared Tex in disgust. "Now I tell you to clear out of heah."

"But, pard, we just want to shee you meet our Jane from Missouri," replied Andy.

"If you-all ain't a lot of four-flushes, I'll eat my chaps!" burst out Tex hotly.

Just then a shrill whistle announced the train.

"You can sneak off now," he went on, "an' leave me to face the music. I always knew I was the only gentleman in Springer's outfit."

The three cowboys did not act upon Tex's sarcastic suggestion, but they hung back, looking at once excited and sheepish and hugely delighted.

The long gray dusty train pulled into the station, and stopped. There was only one passenger for Springer—a woman—and she alighted from the coach near where the cowboys stood waiting. She was not tall and she was much too slight for the heavy valise the porter handed to her.

Tex strode grandly toward her.

"Miss . . . Miss Stacey, ma'am?" he asked, removing his sombrero.

"Yes," she replied. "Are you Mister Owens?"

Evidently the voice was not what Tex had expected and it

disconcerted him.

"No, ma'am, I . . . I'm not Mister Owens," he said. "Please let me take your bag. . . . I'm Tex Dillon, one of Springer's cowboys. An' I've come to meet you . . . an' fetch you out to the ranch."

"Thank you, but I . . . I expected to be met by Mister Owens," she replied.

"Ma'am, there's been a mistake . . . I've got to tell you . . . there ain't any Mister Owens," blurted out Tex manfully.

"Oh!" she said with a little start.

"You see, it was this way," went on the confused cowboy. "One of Springer's cowboys . . . not *me* . . . wrote them letters to you, signin' his name Owens. There ain't no such named cowboy in this county. Your last letter . . . an' here it is . . . fell into my hands . . . all by accident, ma'am, it sure was. I took my three friends heah . . . I took them into my confidence. An' we all came down to meet you."

She moved her head and evidently looked at the strange trio of cowboys Tex had pointed out as his friends. They came forward then, but not eagerly, and they still held to each other. Their condition, not to consider their immense excitement, could not have been lost even upon a tenderfoot from Missouri.

"Please . . . return my . . . my letter," she said, turning again to Tex, and she put out a small gloved hand to take it from him. "Then . . . there is no Mister Frank Owens?"

"No, ma'am, there ain't," replied Tex miserably.

"Is there . . . no . . . no truth in his . . . is there no school-teacher wanted here?" she faltered.

"I think so, ma'am," he replied. "Springer said he needed one. That's what started the advertisement an' the letters to you. You can see the boss an' . . . an' explain. I'm sure it will be all right. He's the grandest fellow. He won't stand for no joke on a poor old schoolmarm."

In his bewilderment he had spoken his thoughts, and that last slip made him look more miserable than ever, and made the boys appear ready to burst.

"Poor old schoolmarm," echoed Miss Stacey. "Perhaps the deceit has not been wholly on one side."

Whereupon she swept aside the enveloping veil to reveal a pale and pretty face. She was young. She had clear gray eyes and a sweet sensitive mouth. Little curls of chestnut hair straggled from under her veil. And she had tiny freckles.

Tex stared at this apparition.

"But you . . . you . . . the letter says she wasn't over forty!" he ejaculated.

"She's not," rejoined Miss Stacey curtly.

Then there were visible and remarkable indications of a transformation in the attitude of the cowboy. But the approach of a stranger suddenly seemed to paralyze him. This fellow was very tall. He strolled up to them. He was booted and spurred. He halted before the group and looked expectantly from the boys to the young woman and back again. But at the moment the four cowboys appeared dumb.

"Are you Mister Springer?" asked Miss Stacey.

"Yes," he replied, and he took off his sombrero. He had a dark frank face and keen eyes.

"I am Jane Stacey," she explained hurriedly. "I'm a school-teacher. I answered an advertisement. And I've come from Missouri because of letters I received from a Mister Frank Owens of Springer's Ranch. This young man met me. He has not been very . . . explicit. I gather that there is no Mister Owens . . . that I'm the victim of a cowboy joke. But he said that Mister Springer won't stand for a joke on a poor old schoolmarm."

"I sure am glad to meet you, Miss Stacey," responded the rancher with the easy Western courtesy that must have been comforting to her. "Please let me see the letters."

She opened a handbag and, searching in it, presently held out several letters.

Springer never even glanced at his stricken cowboys. He took the letters.

"No, not that one," said Miss Stacey, blushing scarlet. "That's one I wrote to Mister Owens, but didn't mail. It's . . . hardly necessary to read that."

While Springer read the others, she looked at him. Presently he asked for the letter she had taken back. Miss Stacey hesitated, then refused. He looked cool, curious, business-like. Then his keen eyes swept over the four cowboys.

"Tex, are you Mister Frank Owens?" he queried sharply.

"I . . . shore . . . ain't," gasped Tex.

Springer asked each of the other boys the same question and received the same maudlin but negative answers. Then he turned again to the girl.

"Miss Stacey, I regret to say that you are indeed the victim of a low-down cowboy trick," he said. "I'd apologize for such a heathen if I knew how. All I can say is I'm sorry."

"Then . . . then there isn't any school to teach . . . any place for me . . . out here?" she asked, and there were tears in her eyes.

"That's another matter," he replied with a winning smile. "Of course there's a place for you. I've wanted a schoolteacher for a long time. Some of the men out at the ranch have kids an' they sure need a teacher."

"Oh, I'm . . . so glad," she murmured in great relief. "I was afraid I'd have to go . . . all the way back. You see, I'm not so strong as I used to be . . . and my doctor advised a change of climate . . . dry Western air."

"You don't look sick," he said with his keen eyes on her. "You look very well to me."

"Oh, indeed, I'm not very strong," she returned quickly. "But

I must confess I wasn't altogether truthful about my age."

"I was wondering about that," he said gravely. There seemed just a glint of a twinkle in his eye. "Not over forty!"

Again she blushed and this time with confusion.

"It wasn't altogether a lie. I was afraid to mention I was only . . . so young. And I wanted to get the position so much . . . I'm a good . . . a competent teacher, unless the scholars are too grown up."

"The scholars you'll have at my ranch are children," he replied. "Well, we'd better be starting if we are to get there before dark. It's a long ride. Is this all your baggage?"

Springer led her over to the buckboard and helped her in, then stowed the valise under the back seat.

"Here, let me put this robe over you," he said. "It'll be dusty. And when we get up on the ridge, it's cold."

At this juncture Tex came to life and he started forward. But Andy and Nevada and Panhandle stood motionlessly, staring at the fresh and now flushed face of the young schoolteacher. Tex untied the halter of the spirited team and they began to prance. He gathered up the reins as if about to mount the buckboard.

"I've got all the supplies an' the mail, Mister Springer," he said cheerfully. "An' I can be startin' at once."

"I'll drive Miss Stacey," replied Springer dryly.

Tex looked blank for a moment. Then Miss Stacey's clear gray eyes seemed to embarrass him. A tinge of red came into his tanned cheek.

"Tex, you can ride my horse home," said the rancher.

"Thet wild stallion of yours!" expostulated the cowboy. "Now, Mister Springer, I shore am afraid of him."

This from the best horseman on the whole range!

Apparently the rancher took Tex seriously. "He sure is wild, Tex, and I know you're a poor hand with a horse. If he throws you, why, you'll have your own horse."

Miss Stacey turned away her eyes. There was a hint of a smile on her lips. Springer got in beside her, and, taking the reins without another glance at his discomfited cowboys, he drove away.

II

A few weeks altered many things at Springer Ranch. There was a marvelous change in the dress and deportment of cowboys off duty. There were some clean and happy and interested children. There was a rather taciturn and lonely young rancher who was given to thoughtful dreams and whose keen eyes watched the little adobe schoolhouse under the cottonwoods. And in Jane Stacey's face a rich bloom and tan had begun to warm out the paleness.

It was not often that Jane left the schoolhouse without meeting one of Springer's cowboys. She met Tex most frequently, and, according to Andy, that fact was because Tex was foreman and could send the boys off to the ends of the range.

And this afternoon Jane encountered the foreman. He was clean-shaven, bright, and eager, a superb figure. Tex had been lucky enough to have a gun with him one day when a rattlesnake frightened the schoolteacher and he had shot the reptile. Miss Stacey had leaned against him in her fright; she had been grateful; she had admired his wonderful skill with a gun and had murmured that a woman always could be sure with such a man. Thereafter Tex packed his gun unmindful of the ridicule of his rivals.

"Miss Stacey, come for a little ride, won't you?" he asked eagerly.

The cowboys had already taught her how to handle a horse and to ride, and, if all they said of her appearance and accomplishment were true, she was indeed worth watching.

"I'm sorry," replied Jane. "I promised Nevada I'd ride with him today." '

"I reckon Nevada is miles an' miles up the valley by now," replied Tex. "He won't be back till long after dark."

"But he made an agreement with me," protested the schoolmistress.

"An' shore he has to work. He's ridin' for Springer, an' I'm foreman of this ranch," said Tex.

"You sent him off on some long chase," averred Jane severely. "Now, didn't you?"

"I shore did. He comes crowin' down to the bunkhouse . . . about how he's goin' to ride with you an' how we-all are not in the runnin'."

"Oh, he did. And what did you say?"

"I says . . . Nevada, I reckon there's a steer mired in the sand up in Cedar Wash. You ride up there an' pull him out."

"And then what did he say?" inquired Jane curiously.

"Why, Miss Stacey, I shore hate to tell you. I didn't think he was so . . . so bad. He just used the most awful language as was ever heard on this heah ranch. Then he rode off."

"But *was* there a steer mired up in the wash?"

"I reckon so," replied Tex, rather shame-facedly. " 'Most always is one."

Jane let scornful eyes rest upon the foreman.

"That was a mean trick," she said.

"There's been worse done to me by him, an' all of them. An' all's fair in love an' war. . . . Will you ride with me?"

"No."

"Why not?"

"Because I think I'll ride off alone up Cedar Wash and help Nevada find that mired steer."

"Miss Stacey, you're shore not goin' to ride off alone. Savvy that?"

"Who'll keep me from it?" demanded Jane with spirit.

"I will. Or any of the boys, for that matter. Springer's orders."

Jane started with surprise, and then blushed rosy red. Tex, also, appeared confused at his disclosure.

"Miss Stacey, I oughtn't have said that. It slipped out. The boss said we needn't tell you, but you were to be watched an' taken care of. It's a wild range. You could get lost or thrown from a horse."

"Mister Springer is very kind and thoughtful," murmured Jane.

"The fact is, this heah ranch is a different place since you came," went on Tex as if emboldened. "An' this beatin' around the bush doesn't suit me. All the boys have lost their haids over you."

"Indeed? How flattering," replied Jane with just a hint of mockery. She was fond of all her admirers, but there were four of them she had not yet forgiven.

The tall foreman was not without spirit.

"It's true all right, as you'll find out pretty quick," he replied. "If you had any eyes, you'd see that cattle raisin' on this heah ranch is about to halt till somethin' is decided. Why, even Springer himself is sweet on you."

"How dare you!" flashed Jane, suddenly aghast.

"I ain't afraid to tell the truth," declared Tex stoutly. "He is. The boys all say so. He's grouchier than ever. He's jealous. Lord, he's jealous! He watches you. . . ."

"Suppose I told him that you dared to say such things?" interrupted Jane, trembling on the verge of strange emotion.

"Why, he'd be tickled to death. He hasn't got nerve enough to tell you himself."

This cowboy, like all his comrades, was hopeless. She was about to attempt to change the conversation when Tex took her into his arms. She struggled—fought with all her might. But he succeeded in kissing her cheek and the tip of her ear. Finally she broke away from him.

"Now . . . ," she panted. "You've done it . . . you've insulted me. Now I'll never ride with you again . . . even speak to you."

"I shore didn't insult you," replied Tex. "Jane . . . won't you marry me?"

"No."

"Won't you be my sweetheart . . . till you care enough to . . . to . . . ?"

"No."

"But, Jane, you'll forgive me, an' be good friends again?"

"Never!"

Jane did not mean all she said. She had come to understand these men of the ranges—their loneliness—their hunger for love. But in spite of her sympathy she needed sometimes to be cold and severe.

"Jane, you owe me a good deal . . . more than you've any idea," said Tex seriously.

"How so?"

"Didn't you ever guess about me?"

"My wildest flight at guessing would never make anything of you, Texas Jack."

"You'd never have been here but for me," he said solemnly.

Jane could only stare at him.

"I meant to tell you long ago. But I shore didn't have nerve. Jane . . . I . . . I was that there letter-writin' feller. I wrote them letters you got. I am Frank Owens."

"No!" exclaimed Jane. She was startled. That matter of Frank Owens had never been cleared up. It had ceased to rankle within her breast, but it had never been forgotten. She looked up earnestly into the big fellow's face. It was like a mask. But she saw through it. He was lying. Almost, she thought, she saw a laugh deep in his eyes.

"I shore am the lucky man who found you a job when you was sick an' needed a change. .... An' you've grown so pretty an' so well . . . you owe all thet to me."

"Tex, if you really were Frank Owens, *that* would make a great difference. I owe him everything. I would . . . but I don't believe you are he."

"It's a sure honest Gospel fact," declared Tex. "I hope to die if it ain't!"

Jane shook her head sadly at his monstrous prevarication.

"I don't believe you," she said, and left him standing there.

It might have been mere coincidence that during the next few days both Nevada and Panhandle waylaid and conveyed to her intelligence by diverse and pathetic arguments the astounding fact that each was Mr. Frank Owens. More likely, however, was it the unerring instinct of lovers who had sensed the importance and significance of this mysterious correspondent's part in bringing health and happiness into Jane Stacey's life. She listened to them with anger and sadness and amusement at their deceit, and she had the same answer for both: "I don't believe you."

And through these machinations of the cowboys Jane had begun to have vague and sweet and disturbing suspicions of her own as to the real identity of that mysterious cowboy, Frank Owens. Andy had originality as well as daring. He would have completely deceived Jane if she had not happened, by the merest accident, to discover the relation between him and certain love letters she had begun to find in her desk. She was deceived at first, for the typewriting of these was precisely like that in the letters of Frank Owens. She had been suddenly aware of a wild start of rapture. That had given place to a shameful open-eyed realization of the serious condition of her own heart. But she happened to discover in Andy the writer of these missives, and her dream was shattered, if not forgotten. Andy certainly would not carry love letters to her that he did not write. He had merely learned to use the same typewriter and at opportune times he had slipped the letters into her desk. Jane now began to have her own little aching haunting secret that was so hard to put out of her mind. Every letter and every hint of Frank Owens made her remember. Therefore she decided to put a check to Andy's sly double-dealing. She addressed a note to him and wrote:

> *Dear Andy,*
>
> *That day at the train when you thought I was a poor old schoolmarm you swore you were not Frank Owens. Now you swear you are! If you were a man who knew what truth is, you'd have a chance. But now. . . . No! You are a monster of iniquity. I don't believe you.*

She left the note in plain sight where she always found his letters in her desk. The next morning the note was gone. And so was Andy. She did not see him for three days.

It came about that a dance to be held at Beacon during the late summer was something Jane could not very well avoid. She had not attended either of the cowboy dances that had been given since her arrival. This next one, however, appeared to be an annual affair, at which all the ranching fraternity for miles around would be in attendance. Jane was wild to go. But it developed that she could not escape the escort of any one of her cowboy admirers without alienating the others. And she began to see the visions of this wonderful dance fade away when Springer accosted her.

"Who's the lucky cowboy to take you to our dance?" he asked.

"He's as mysterious and doubtful as Mister Frank Owens," replied Jane.

"Oh, you still remember him," said the rancher, his keen dark eyes quizzically on her.

"Indeed, I do," sighed Jane.

"Too bad. He was a villain. . . . But you don't mean you haven't been asked to go?"

"They've all asked me . . . that's the trouble."

"I see. But you mustn't miss it. It'd be pleasant for you to meet some of the ranchers and their wives. Suppose you go with me?"

"Oh, Mister Springer, I . . . I'd be delighted," replied Jane.

"Thank you. Then it's settled. I must be in town all that day on cattle business . . . next Friday. I'll ask the Hartwells to stop here for you, an' drive you in."

He seemed gravely, kindly interested as always, yet there was something in his eyes that interfered with the regular beating of Jane's heart. She could not forget what the cowboys had told her, even if she dared not believe it.

Jane spent much of the remaining leisure hours working on a gown to wear at this dance that promised so much. And because of the labor, she saw little of the cowboys. Tex was highly offended with her and would not deign to notice her anyhow. She wondered what would happen at the dance. She was a little fearful, too, because she had already learned of what fire and brimstone these cowboys were made. So dreaming and conjecturing, now amused and again gravely pensive, Jane awaited the eventful night.

The Hartwells turned out to be nice people whose little girl was one of Jane's pupils. That, and their evident delight in Jane's appearance, gave the adventure a last thrilling anticipation. Jane had been afraid to trust her own judgment as to how she looked. On the drive townward, through the crisp fall gloaming, while listening to the chatter of the children, and the talk of the elder Hartwells, she could not help wondering what Springer would think of her in the beautiful new gown.

They arrived late, according to her escorts. The drive to town was sixteen miles, but it had seemed short to Jane. "Reckon it's just as well for you an' the children," said Mrs. Hartwell to Jane. "These dances last from seven to seven."

"No!" exclaimed Jane.

"They sure do."

"Well, I'm a tenderfoot from Missouri. But that's not going to keep me from having a wonderful time."

"You will, dear, unless the cowboys fight over you, which is likely. But at least there won't be any shootin'. My husband an' Springer are both on the committee an' they won't admit any gun-totin' cowpunchers."

Here Jane had concrete evidence of something she had begun to suspect. These careless love-making cowboys might be dangerous. It thrilled while it repelled her.

Jane's first sight of that dance hall astonished her. It was a big barn-like room, roughly raftered and sided, decorated enough with colored bunting to take away the bareness. The lamps were not bright, but there were enough of them to give collectively a good light. The volume of sound amazed her. Music and trample of boots, gay laughter, deep voices of men all seemed to merge into a loud hum. A swaying, wheeling horde of dancers circled past her. No more time then was accorded her to clarify the spectacle, for Springer suddenly confronted her. He seemed different somehow. Perhaps it was an absence of ranchers' corduroys and boots, if Jane needed assurance of what she had dreamed of and hoped for. She had it in his frank admiration.

"Sure it's somethin' fine for Bill Springer to have the prettiest girl here," he said.

"Thank you . . . but, Mister Springer . . . I sadly fear you were a cowboy before you became a rancher," she replied archly.

"Sure I was. An' that you may find out." He laughed. "Of course, I could never come up to . . . say . . . Frank Owens. But let's dance. I shall have little enough of you in this outfit."

So he swung her into the circle of dancers. Jane found him easy to dance with, although he was far from expert. It was a jostling mob, and she soon acquired a conviction that, if her gown did outlast the whole dance, her feet never would. Springer took his dancing seriously and had little to say. Jane felt strange and uncertain with him. Then soon she became aware of the cessation of hum and movement.

"Sure that was the best dance I ever had," said Springer with something of radiance in his dark face. "An' now I must lose you to this outfit comin'."

Manifestly he meant his cowboys Tex, Nevada, Panhandle, and Andy who presented themselves four abreast, shiny of hair and face.

"Good luck," he whispered. "If you get into trouble, let me know."

What he meant quickly dawned upon Jane. Right there it began. She saw there was absolutely no use in trying to avoid or refuse these young men. The wisest and safest course was to surrender, which she did.

"Boys, don't all talk at once. I can dance with only one of you at a time. So I'll take you in alphabetical order. I'm a poor old schoolmarm from Missouri. It'll be Andy, Nevada, Panhandle, and Tex."

Despite their protests she held rigidly to this rule. Each one of the cowboys took shameless advantage of his opportunity. Outrageously as they all hugged her, Tex was the worst offender. She tried to stop dancing, but he carried her along as if she had been a child. He was rapt, and yet there seemed a devil in him.

"Tex . . . how dare you," panted Jane, when at last the dance ended.

"Wal, I reckon I'd aboot dare anythin' for you, Jane," he replied, towering over her.

"You ought to be . . . ashamed," went on Jane. "I'll not dance with you again."

"Aw, now," he pleaded.

"I won't, Tex . . . so there. You're no gentleman."

"Ahuh!" he ejaculated, drawing himself up stiffly. "All right, I'll go out an' get drunk, an', when I come back, I'll clean out this heah hall."

"Tex! Don't go!" she called hurriedly as he started to stride away. "I'll take that back. I will give you another dance . . . if you promise to . . . to behave."

Then she got rid of him, and was carried off by Mrs. Hartwell to be introduced to ranchers and their wives, to girls and their escorts. She found herself a center of admiring eyes. She promised more dances than she could remember or keep.

Her new partner was a tall handsome cowboy named Jones. She did not know quite what to make of him. But he was an unusually good dancer, and he did not hold her so that she had difficulty in breathing. He talked all the time. He was witty and engaging, and he had a most subtly flattering tongue. Jane could not fail to grasp that he might even be worse than Tex, but at least he did not make love to her with physical violence. She enjoyed that dance and admitted the singular forceful charm about this Mr. Jones. If he was a little too bold of glance and somehow primitively assured and debonair, she passed it by in the excitement and joy of the hour, and in the certainty that she was now a long way from Missouri. Jones demanded rather than begged for another dance, and, although she laughingly explained her predicament in regard to partners, he said he would come after her anyhow.

Then followed several dances with new partners, between which Jane became more than ever the center of attraction. It all went to her head like wine. She was having a perfectly wonderful time. Jones claimed her again, in fact whirled her out on the floor, and it seemed then that the irresistible rush of the dancers was similar to her sensations. Twice again before the supper hour at midnight she found herself dancing with Jones. How he managed it she did not know. He just took her, carried her off by storm. Jane did not awaken to this unpardonable conduct of hers until she discovered that a little while before she had promised Tex his second dance, and then she had given it to Jones, or at least had danced it with him. What could she do when he walked right off with her? It was a glimpse of Tex's face, as she was being whirled around in Jones's arms, that filled Jane with remorse.

Then came the supper hour. It was a gala occasion, for which evidently the children had heroically kept awake. Jane enjoyed the children immensely. She sat with the numerous Hartwells, all of whom were most kindly attentive to her. Jane wondered why Mr. Springer did not put in an appearance, but considered his absence due to numerous duties.

When the supper hour ended and the people were stirring about the hall, and the men were tuning up, Jane caught sight of Andy. He looked rather pale and sick. Jane tried to catch his eye, but failing that she went to him.

"Andy, please find Tex for me. I owe him a dance, and I'll give him the very first, unless Mister Springer comes for it."

Andy regarded her with an aloofness totally new to her.

"Wal, I'll tell him. But I reckon Tex ain't presentable just now. All of us are through dancin' tonight."

"What's happened?" queried Jane, swift to divine trouble.

"There's been a little fight."

"Oh, no!" cried Jane. "Who? What? Andy, tell me."

"Wal, when you cut Tex's dance for Beady Jones, you sure put our outfit in bad," replied Andy coldly. "At thet there wouldn't have been anythin' come of it here if Beady Jones hadn't got to shootin' off his chin. Tex slapped his face an' thet sure started a fight. Beady licked Tex, too, I'm sorry to say. He's a pretty bad customer, Beady is, an' he's bigger'n Tex. Wal, we had a hell of a time keepin' Nevada out of it. Thet would have been an uneven fight. I'd like to have seen it. But we kept them apart till Springer come out. An' what the boss said to thet outfit was sure aplenty. Beady Jones kept talkin' back, nasty like . . . you know he was once foreman for us . . . till Springer got good an' mad. An' he said . . . 'Jones, I fired you once because you was a little too slick for our outfit, an' I'll tell you this, if it comes to a pinch, I'll give you the damnedest thrashin' any smart-aleck cowboy ever got!' Gee, the boss was riled. It sort of surprised me, an' tickled me pink. You can bet that shut Beady Jones's loud mouth."

After that rather lengthy speech Andy left her unceremoniously standing there alone. She was not alone long, but it was long enough for her to feel bitter dissatisfaction with herself.

Jane looked for Springer, hoping yet fearing he would come to her. But he did not. She had another uninterrupted dizzy round of dancing until her strength failed. At 4:00 A.M. she was scarcely able to walk. Her pretty dress was torn and mussed; her white stockings were no longer white; her slippers were worn ragged. And her feet were dead. From that time she sat with Mrs. Hartwell, looking on and trying to keep awake. The wonderful dance, that had begun so promisingly, had ended sadly for her.

At length the exodus began, although Jane did not see any dancers leaving. She went out with the Hartwells, to be received by Springer, who had evidently made arrangements for their leaving. He was decidedly cool to Jane.

All through the long ride out to the ranch he never addressed her or looked toward her. Daylight came, cold and gray to Jane.

She felt crushed.

Springer's sister and the matronly housekeeper were waiting for them, with cheery welcome, and invitation to a hot breakfast.

Presently Jane found herself momentarily alone with the rancher.

"Miss Stacey," he said in a voice she had never heard, "your flirtin' with Beady Jones made trouble for the Springer outfit."

"Mister Springer!" she exclaimed, her head going up.

"Excuse me," he returned in cutting dry tone that recalled Tex. Indeed, this Westerner was a cowboy, the same as those who rode for him, only a little older, and therefore more reserved and careful of speech. "If it wasn't that . . . then you were much taken with Mister Beady Jones."

"If that was anybody's business, it might have appeared so," she retorted, tingling all over with some feeling she could not control.

"Sure. But are you denyin' it?" he queried soberly, eying her with grave wonder and disapproval. It was this more than his question that roused hot anger and contrariness in Jane.

"I admired Mister Jones very much," replied Jane. "He was a splendid dancer. He did not maul me like a bear. I really had a chance to breathe during my dances with him. Then, too, he could talk."

Springer bowed with dignity. His dark face paled. It began to dawn upon Jane that there was something intense in the moment. She began to repent of her hasty pride.

"Thanks," he said. "Please excuse my impertinence. I see you have found your Mister Frank Owens in this cowboy Jones, an' it sure is not my place to say any more."

"But . . . but . . . Mister Springer . . . ," faltered Jane, quite unstrung by that amazing speech. The rancher, however, bowed again, and left her. Jane felt too miserable and weary for anything but rest. She went to her room, and, flinging off her hateful finery, she crawled into bed, a very perplexed and distraught young woman.

About midafternoon Jane awakened greatly refreshed and relieved and strangely repentant. She dressed prettily and went out, not quite sure of or satisfied with herself. She walked up and down the long porch of the ranch house, gazing out over the purple range on to the black belt of forest up the mountains. How beautiful this Arizona! She loved it. Could she ever go away? The thought reposed, to stay before her consciousness. She invaded the kitchen, where the matronly housekeeper, who was fond of her, gave her wild-turkey sandwiches and cookies and sweet rich milk. While Jane mitigated her hunger, the woman gossiped about the cowboys and Springer, and the information she imparted renewed Jane's concern.

From the kitchen Jane went out into the courtyard, and naturally, as always, gravitated toward the corrals and barns. Springer appeared, in company with a rancher Jane did not know. She expected Springer to stop her for a few pleasant words as he always did. This time, however, he merely touched his sombrero and passed on. Jane felt the incident almost as a slight. It hurt her.

Then she went on down the lane, very thoughtful. A cloud had appeared above the horizon of her happy life there at the Springer Ranch. The lane opened out into the wide square, around which were the gates to corrals, entrances to barns, the forge, granaries, and the commodious bunkhouse of the cowboys.

Jane's sharp eyes caught sight of the boys before they espied her. And when she looked up again, every lithe back was turned. They allowed her to pass without any apparent knowledge of her existence. This was unprecedented. It offended Jane bitterly. She knew she was unreasonable, but could not or would not help it. She strolled on down to the pasture gate, and watched the colts and calves. Upon her return, she passed closer to the cowboys. But again they apparently did not see her. Jane added resentment to her wounded vanity and pride. Yet even then a still small voice tormented. She went back to her room, meaning to read or sew, or do schoolwork. But instead she cried.

Springer did not put in an appearance at the dinner table, and that was the last straw for Jane. She realized she had made a mess of her wonderful opportunity there. But those stupid fiery cowboys! This sensitive Westerner! How could she know how to take them? The worst of it was that she was genuinely fond of the cowboys. And as for the rancher—her mind seemed vague and unreliable about him, but she said she hated him.

Next day was Sunday. Heretofore every Sunday had been a full day for Jane. This one bade fair to be empty. Company came as usual, neighbors from nearby ranches. The cowboys were off duty and other cowboys visited them.

Jane's attention was attracted by sight of a superb horseman riding up the lane to the ranch house. He seemed familiar, but she could not place him. What a picture he made as he dismounted, slick and shiny, booted and spurred, to doff his huge sombrero. Jane heard him ask for Miss Stacey. Then she recognized him. Beady Jones! She was at once horrified, and something else she could not name. She remembered now he had asked if he might call Sunday and she had certainly not refused. But for him to come after the fight with Tex and the bitter scene with Springer! It seemed an unparalleled affront. What manner of man was this cowboy Jones? He certainly did not lack courage. But more to the point—what idea had he of her? Jane rose to the occasion. She had let herself in for this, and she would see it through, come what might. Looming disaster stimulated her. She would show these indifferent, deceitful, fire-spirited, incomprehensible cowboys. She would let Springer see she, indeed, had taken Beady Jones for Mr. Frank Owens.

To that end Jane made her way down the porch to greet her cowboy visitor. She made herself charming and gracious, and carried off the embarrassing situation—for Springer was present—as if it were perfectly natural. And she led Jones to one of the rustic benches down the porch.

Jane meant to gauge him speedily, if that were possible. While she made conversation, she brought to bear all that she possessed of intuition and discernment, now especially excited. The situation here was easy for her.

Naturally Jones resembled the cowboys she knew. The same range and life had developed him. But he lacked certain things she liked so much in Tex and Nevada. He was a superb animal. She had reluctantly to admire his cool easy boldness in a situation certainly perilous for him. But then he had reasoned, of course, that she would be his protection. She did not fail to note that he carried a gun inside his embroidered vest.

Manifest, indeed, was it that young Jones felt he had made a conquest. He was the most forceful and bold person Jane had ever met, quite incapable of appreciating her as a lady. Soon he waxed ardent. Jane was accustomed to the sentimental talk of cowboys, but this fellow was neither amusing nor interesting. He was dangerous. When Jane pulled her hand, by main force, free from his, and said she was not accustomed to allow men such privileges, he grinned at her like a handsome devil.

"Sure, sweetheart, you have missed a heap of fun," he said. "An' I reckon I'll have to break you in."

Jane could not feel insulted at this brazen lout, but she certainly raged at herself. Her instant impulse was to excuse herself and abruptly leave him. But Springer was close by. She had caught his dark wandering covert glances. And the cowboys were at the other end of the long porch. Jane feared another fight. She had brought this upon herself, and she must stick it out. The ensuing hour was an increasing torment. At last it seemed she could not bear the false situation any longer, and, when Jones again importuned her to meet him out on horseback, she stooped to deception to end the interview. She really did not concentrate her attention on his plan or take stock of what she'd agreed to, but she got rid of him with lax dignity before Springer and the others. After that, she did not have the courage to stay out and face them. How bitterly she had disappointed the rancher! Jane stole off to the darkness and loneliness of her room. There, however, she was not above peeping out from behind her window blind at the cowboys. They had grown immeasurably in her estimation. Alas! No doubt they were through with the little tenderfoot schoolmarm from Missouri.

III

The school teaching went on just the same, and the cowboys thawed out and Springer returned somewhat to his kindliness, but Jane missed something from her work and in them. At heart she grieved. Would it ever be the same again? What had happened? She had only been an emotional little tenderfoot unused to Western ways. Indeed, she had not failed, at least in gratitude and affection, although now it seemed they would never know.

There came a day when Jane rode off alone toward the hills. She forgot the risk and the admonitions of the cowboys. She wanted to be alone to think. Her happiness had sustained a subtle change. Her work, the children, the friends she had made, even the horse she loved were no longer all-sufficient. Something had come over her. She tried to persuade herself that she was homesick or morbid. But she was not honest with herself and knew it.

It was late fall, but the sun was warm that afternoon, and it was the season when little wind prevailed. Before her lay the valley range, a green-gray expanse dotted with cattle, and beyond it the cedared foothills rose, and above them loomed the dark beckoning mountains. Her horse was fast and liked to run with her. She loved him and the open range, with the rushing breeze on her face, and all that clear lonely vast and silent world before her. Never would she return to live in the crowded cities again, with their horde of complaining people. She had found health and life—and something that wrung her heart and stung her cheek.

She rode fast till her horse was hot and she was out of breath. Then she slowed down. The foothills seemed so close now. But they were not really close. Still she could smell the fragrant dry cedar aroma on the air.

Then for the first time she looked back toward the ranch. It was a long way off—ten miles—a mere green spot in the gray. And there was a horseman coming. As usual someone of the cowboys had observed her, let her think she had slipped away, and was now following her. Today it angered Jane. She wanted to be alone. She could take care of herself. And as was usual with her she used her quirt on the horse. He broke into a gallop. She did not look back again for a long time. When she did, it was to discover that the horseman had not only gained, but was now quite close to her. Jane looked hard, but she could not recognize the rider. Once she imagined it was Tex, and again Andy. It did not make any difference which one of the cowboys it was. She was angry, and, if he caught up with her, he would be sorry.

Jane rode the longest and fastest race she had ever ridden. She reached the low foothills, and, without heeding the fact that she would at once become lost, she entered the cedars and began to climb. She ascended a hill, went down the slope, up a ravine, to climb again. At times her horse had to walk, and then

she heard her pursuer breaking through the cedars. He had to
trail her by her horse's tracks, and so she was able to keep in
the lead. It was not long until Jane realized she was lost, but she
did not care. She rode up and down and around for an hour
until she was thoroughly tired out, and then up on top of a
foothill she reined in her horse and waited to give this pursuer a
piece of her mind.

What was her amaze, when she heard a thud of hoofs and
cracking of branches in the opposite direction from which she
expected her pursuer, to see a rider emerge from the cedars and
trot his horse toward her. Jane needed only a second glance to
recognize Beady Jones. Surely she had met him by chance. Suddenly she knew that he was not the pursuer she had been so
angrily aware of. Jones's horse was white. That checked her
mounting anger.

Jones rode straight at her, and, as he came close, Jane saw his
bold dark face and gleaming eyes. Instantly she realized she had
been mad to ride so far into the wild country, to expose herself
to something from which the cowboys had always tried to save
her.

"Howdy, sweetheart," said Jones in his cool, devil-may-care
way. "Reckon it took you a long time to meet me as you
promised."

"I didn't ride out to meet you, Mister Jones," replied Jane
spiritedly. "I know I agreed to something or other, but even
then I didn't mean it."

"Yes, I had a hunch you was playin' with me," he returned
darkly, riding right up against her horse.

He reached out a long gloved hand and grasped her arm.

"What do you mean, sir?" demanded Jane, trying to wrench
free.

"Sure I mean a lot," he said grimly. "You stood for the love-
makin' of that Springer outfit. Now you're goin' to get a taste of

somethin' not so mushy."

"Let go of me . . . you . . . you ruffian!" cried Jane, struggling fiercely. She was both furious and terrified. But she seemed to be a child in the grasp of a giant.

"Hell! Your fightin' will only make it interestin'. Come here, you deceitful little cat."

And he lifted her out of her saddle over in front of him. Jane's horse, that had been frightened and plunging, ran away into the cedars. Then gently the cowboy proceeded to embrace Jane. She managed to keep her mouth from contact with his, but he kissed her face and neck, kisses that seemed to pollute her.

"Jane, I'm ridin' out of this country for good," he said. "An' I've just been waitin' for this chance. You bet you'll remember Beady Jones."

Jane realized that this Jones would stop at nothing. Frantically she fought to get away from him and to pitch herself to the ground. She screamed. She beat and tore at him. She scratched his face till the blood flowed. And as her struggles increased with her fright, she gradually slipped down between him and the pommel of his saddle with head hanging down on one side and her feet on the other. This was awkward and painful, but infinitely preferable to being crushed in his arms. He was riding off with her as if she had been an empty sack. Suddenly Jane's hands, while trying to hold onto something to lessen the severe jolt of her position, came in contact with Jones's gun. Dare she draw it and shoot him? Then all at once her ears filled with the tearing gallop of another horse. Inverted as she was, she was able to see and recognize Springer ride right at Jones and yell piercingly.

Next she felt Jones's hard jerk at his gun. But Jane had hold of it, and suddenly she made her little hands like steel. The fierce energy with which Jones wrestled to draw his gun threw

Jane from the saddle. And when she dropped clear of the horse, the gun came with her.

"Hands up, Beady!" she heard Springer call out as she lay momentarily face down in the dust. Then she struggled to her knees, and crawled to get away from proximity to the horses. She still clung to the heavy gun. And when breathless and almost collapsing she fell back on the ground, and saw Jones with his hands above his head and Springer on foot with leveled gun.

"Sit tight, cowboy," ordered the rancher in hard tone. "It'll take damn' little to make me bore you." Then, while still covering Jones, evidently ready for any sudden move, Springer spoke again. "Jane, did you come out to meet this cowboy?"

"Oh, no! How can you ask that?" cried Jane, almost sobbing.

"She's a liar, boss," spoke up Jones coolly. "She let me make love to her. An' she agreed to ride out an' meet me. Wal, it sure took her a spell, an', when she did come, she was shy on the love-makin's. I was packin' her off to scare some sense into her when you rode in."

"Beady, I know your way with women. You can save your breath, for I've a hunch you're goin' to need it."

"Mister Springer," faltered Jane, getting to her knees, "I . . . I was foolishly taken with this cowboy . . . at first. Then . . . that Sunday after the dance when he called on me at the ranch . . . I saw through him then. I heartily despised him. To get rid of him I did say I'd meet him. But I never meant to. Then I forgot it. Today I rode for the first time. I saw someone following me and thought it must be Tex or one of the boys. Finally I waited and presently Jones rode up to me. . . . And, Mister Springer, he . . . he grabbed me off my horse . . . and handled me most brutally . . . shamefully. I fought him with all my might, but what could I do?"

Springer's face changed markedly during Jane's long explanation. Then he threw his gun on the ground in front of Jane.

"Jones, I'm goin' to beat you half to death," he said grimly, and, leaping at the cowboy, he jerked him out of the saddle until he was sprawling on the ground. Next Springer threw aside his sombrero, his vest, his spurs. But he kept on his gloves. The cowboy rose to one knee, and he measured the distance between him and Springer, and then the gun that lay on the ground. Suddenly he sprang toward it. But Springer intercepted him with a powerful kick that tripped Jones and laid him flat.

"Jones, you're sure about as low-down as they come," he said in dark scorn. "I've got to be satisfied with beatin' you when I ought to kill you."

"Ahuh! Wal, boss, it ain't any safe bet thet you can beat me," returned Jones sullenly while he got up.

As they rushed together, Jane had wit enough to pick up the gun, and then with it and Jones's, to get back to a safe distance. She wanted to run away out of sight. But she could neither do that nor keep her fascinated gaze from the combatants. Even in her distraught condition she could see that the cowboy, fierce and active and strong as he was, could not hold his own with Springer. They fought over all the open space, and crashed into the cedars, and out again. The time came when Jones was on the ground about as much as he was erect. Bloody, disheveled, beaten, he kept on trying to stem the onslaught of blows.

Suddenly he broke off a dead branch of cedar and, brandishing it, rushed at the rancher. Jane uttered a cry, closed her eyes, and sank down. She heard fierce imprecations and sodden blows. When at length she opened her eyes in terror, fearing something dreadful, she saw Springer erect, wiping his face, and Jones lying prone on the ground.

Then Jane saw him go to his horse, untie a canteen from the saddle, remove his bloody gloves, and wash his face with a wet scarf. Next he poured some water on Jones's face.

"Come on, Jane!" he called. "Reckon it's all over."

Then he tied the bridle of Jones's horse to a cedar and, leading his own animal, turned to meet Jane.

"I want to compliment you on gettin' that cowboy's gun," he said warmly. "But for that, there'd sure have been somethin' bad. I'd have had to kill him, Jane. Here, give me the guns. . . . You poor little tenderfoot from Missouri. No, not tenderfoot any longer, you became a Westerner today."

His face was bruised and cut, his dress dirty and bloody, but he did not appear the worse for that fight. Jane found her legs scarcely able to support her, and she had apparently lost her voice.

"Let us put you on my saddle till we find your horse," he said, and lifted her lightly as a feather to a seat crosswise. Then he walked with a hand on the bridle.

Jane saw him examining the ground, evidently searching for horse tracks. "Ha! Here we are." And he led off in another direction through the cedars. Soon Jane espied her horse, calmly nibbling at the bleached grass. In a few moments she was back in her own saddle, beginning to recover somewhat from her distress. But she divined that as fast as she recovered from one set of emotions she was going to be tormented by another.

"There's a good cold spring down here in the rocks," remarked Springer. "I think you need a drink, an' so do I."

They rode down the sunny cedar slopes, into a shady ravine skirted by pines, and up to some mossy cliffs from which a spring gushed forth.

Jane was now in the throes of thrilling, bewildering conjectures and fears. Why had Springer followed her? Why had he not sent one of the cowboys? Why did she feel so afraid and foolish? He had always been courteous and kind and thoughtful, at least until she had offended so egregiously. And here he was now. He had fought for her. Would she ever forget? Her heart began to pound. And when he dismounted to take her off her horse, she knew it was to see a scarlet and telltale face.

"Mister Springer, I . . . I thought you were Tex . . . or somebody," she said.

He laughed as he took off his sombrero. His face was warm, and the cuts were still bleeding a little.

"You sure can ride," he replied. "And that's a good little pony."

He loosened the cinches on the horses. Jane managed to hide some of her confusion.

"Won't you walk around a little?" he asked. "It'll rest you. We are fifteen miles from home."

"So far?"

Then presently he lifted her up and stood beside her with a hand on her horse. He looked up frankly into her face. The keen eyes were softer than usual. He seemed so fine and strong and splendid. She was afraid of her eyes and looked away.

"When the boys found you were gone, they all saddled up to find you," he said. "But I asked them if they didn't think the boss ought to have one chance. So they let me come."

Something happened to Jane's heart just then. She was suddenly overwhelmed by a strange happiness that she must hide, but could not. It seemed there was a long silence. She felt Springer there, but she could not look at him.

"Do you like it out here in the West?" he asked presently.

"Oh, I love it! I'll never want to leave it," she replied impulsively.

"I reckon I'm glad to hear that."

Then there fell another silence. He pressed closer to her and seemed now to be leaning on the horse. She wondered if he heard the weird knocking of her heart against her side.

"Will you be my wife an' stay here always?" he asked simply. "I'm in love with you. I've been lonely since my mother died.

. . . You'll sure have to marry some one of us. Because, as Tex says, if you don't, ranchin' can't go on much longer. These boys don't seem to get anywhere with you. Have I any chance . . . Jane . . . ?"

He possessed himself of her gloved hand and gave her a gentle pull. Jane knew it was gentle because she scarcely felt it. Yet it had irresistible power. She was swayed by that gentle pull. She was slipping sidewise in her saddle. She was sliding into his arms.

A little later he smiled up at her and said: "Jane, they call me Bill for short. Same as they call me boss. But my two front names are Frank Owens."

"Oh!" cried Jane, startled. "Then you . . . you . . . ?"

"Yes, I'm the guilty one," he replied happily. "It happened this way. My bedroom, you know, is next to my office. I often heard the boys poundin' the typewriter. I had a hunch they were up to some trick. So I spied upon them . . . heard about Frank Owens an' the letters to the little schoolmarm. At Beacon I got the postmistress to give me your address. An', of course, I intercepted some of your letters. It sure has turned out great."

"I . . . I don't know about you or those terrible cowboys," replied Jane dubiously. "How did *they* happen on the name Frank Owens?"

"Sure, that's a stumper. I reckon they put a job up on me."

"Frank . . . tell me . . . did *you* write the . . . the love letters?" she asked appealingly. "There were two kinds of letters. That's what I could never understand."

"Jane, I reckon I did," he confessed. "Somethin' about your little notes just won me. Does that make it all right?"

"Yes, Frank, I reckon it does," she returned, leaning down to kiss him.

"Let's ride back home an' tell the boys," said Springer gaily.

"The joke's sure on them. I've corralled the little schoolmarm from Missouri."

ABOUT THE AUTHOR

Zane Grey was born Pearl Zane Gray at Zanesville, Ohio in 1872. He was graduated from the University of Pennsylvania in 1896 with a degree in dentistry. He practiced in New York City while striving to make a living by writing. He married Lina Elise Roth in 1905 and with her financial assistance he published his first novel himself, *Betty Zane* (1903). Closing his dental office, the Greys moved into a cottage on the Delaware River, near Lackawaxen, Pennsylvania. Grey took his first trip to Arizona in 1907 and, following his return, wrote *The Heritage of the Desert* (1910). The profound effect that the desert had had on him was so vibrantly captured that it still comes alive for a reader. Grey couldn't have been more fortunate in his choice of a mate. Trained in English at Hunter College, Lina Grey proofread every manuscript Grey wrote, polished his prose, and later she managed their financial affairs. Grey's early novels were serialized in pulp magazines, but by 1918 he had graduated to the slick magazine market. Motion picture rights brought in a fortune and, with 109 films based on his work, Grey set a record yet to be equaled by any other author. Zane Grey was not a realistic writer, but rather one who charted the interiors of the soul through encounters with the wilderness. He provided characters no less memorable than one finds in Balzac, Dickens, or Thomas Mann, and they have a vital story to tell. "There was so much unexpressed feeling that could not be entirely portrayed," Loren Grey, Grey's younger son and a noted psychologist, once recalled, "that, in later years, he would weep when re-reading one of his own books." Perhaps, too, closer to the mark, Zane Grey may have wept at how his attempts at being truthful to his muse had so often been essentially altered by his editors, so that no one might ever be able to read his stories as he had intended them. It may be said of Zane Grey that, more than mere adventure tales, he fashioned psycho-dramas about the odyssey of the human soul. If his stories seem not always to be of the stuff of the mundane world, without what his stories do touch, the human world has little meaning—which may go a long way to explain the hold he has had on an enraptured reading public ever since his first Western novel in 1910.